VINCENT
IN
WONDERLAND

PREQUEL TO
THE
WORLDS
NEXT DOOR

C. E. WHITE

Vincent in Wonderland by C.E. White

ISBN 978-0-9912329-9-4

CWM Publishing

cewhitebooks@gmail.com
www.cewhitebooks.com
www.instagram.com/cewhitebooks
www.facebook.com/cewhitebooks
www.twitter.com/cewhitebooks

First Edition, July 2019

Cover image by M.S. Corley – www.mscorley.com
Interior design by Kevin G. Summers – literaryoutlaw.com
Illustrations by Todd Holley – onyxai@aol.com

To anyone who has ever felt like the world doesn't want what you have to offer— give it anyway.

To Michaela—

Be
extra-ordinary!

C. E. White

CHAPTER ONE

What I am in the eyes of most people—a nonentity, an eccentric, or an unpleasant person—somebody who has no position in society and will never have—in short, the lowest of the low. All right, then. Even if that were absolutely true, then I should like to show by my work what such an eccentric, such a nobody, has in his heart.

—Vincent van Gogh

Zundert, The Netherlands - 1864

Vincent skipped every other step down the stairs in a mad dash from his bedroom. He'd seen two of his father's most long-winded parishioners walking up the path to the parsonage, and he didn't want to get stuck listening to the same stories they repeated week after week. He was terrible at pretending to be interested.

He grabbed his blue bottle in case he saw any interesting bugs and fled out the back door just as the guests knocked at the front. He ran out of the garden,

1

through the moor, and into the marsh. Each footfall sent mud splattering everywhere, and he loved it. Mud was real—the stuff underneath, hidden by the grass and the flowers. His parents only seemed to care about how everything looked on top—everything, including him.

He reached the bank of the big creek and plopped down on a sandy patch of ground, chest heaving from his run. Beetles scooted across the surface of the water, and a heron landed with a faint splash in the muddy shallows of the shore opposite him. He ran his hands across the grains of sand, enjoying the feel of the rough grit.

The iridescent green of a water bug glinted in the sunlight, and Vincent reached for his bottle, then rose to his knees and leaned out to capture it. It danced out of reach, and he sank back to watch it skate away.

A rustling near the far hillock drew his attention, and a head bobbed into view. He frowned as the face appeared.

Hendrik.

At thirteen, Hendrik had two years and about a foot in height on Vincent. Hendrik pointed in his direction as three more sets of shoulders topped the rise. Vincent couldn't make out the words, but Hendrik's mouth moved, and an echo of laughter reached him. The town boys always terrorized Vincent if they could, calling him strange, taking—and often breaking—his things, and shoving him in the dirt.

Vincent stood, vacillating between the desire to defend himself and the desire to escape. He noted the wide brook behind him and opted to run. He'd certainly end up in the water if they cornered him on the shore.

He took off running, not toward home, but in the direction of the barrow mound on the moor. Most people were too superstitious to crawl into the burial mounds, but Vincent had investigated this one a long time ago and never found anything. It was partially caved in and barely big enough for him to hide within, but nothing marked the opening while the summer vines overgrew it. He didn't think the boys would find him if he reached it ahead of them, and he was fast. This, he knew from experience.

When he topped the next hill, he rounded through the trees so he could approach the barrow mound from the back. It was the long way around, but if he took the shortest route, he'd still be in plain sight when the other boys came over the knoll. This way, he'd come to the entrance from the rear, and they'd never know where he went.

He sped on, branches whipping his face, thankful the mossy ground under the trees muffled his footsteps. He stopped at the edge of the tree line, breathing hard and checking for his tormentors. The dash from here to the barrow would put him out in the open. He ran as quickly and silently as he could toward the hillock and never stumbled. He knew the moor as he knew his own mother's face.

The underbrush crashed with the other boys' approach—they certainly didn't attempt any stealth—but the swell of the barrow rose before him, and they were on the far side of it. He reached it and knelt in front of the opening, carefully parting the brush that hid it to climb in. He rearranged the vines covering the hole, then backed in as far as he could—thankfully, far enough that the light from the opening did not touch him.

Their voices reached him now. "Did you see where he went?"

"Back to his mommy, I bet."

"Just like the little coward to run away!"

That last one was Hendrik's voice.

Their lumbering footsteps grew louder and louder then passed into silence as they entered the trees. He didn't think they would come back to look for him. They didn't seem to have the patience for an actual search.

Vincent stayed where he was, though, relaxing into the cool dirt, taking in the dank smell of the earth. The light fell in patches across the ground in front of him, flickering as a breeze tickled the leaves.

He knew someone must've been buried here at some point, but that didn't bother him. He actually enjoyed the dark stillness inside the barrow. He found it comforting.

The dead expect nothing of me.

Suddenly, the earth shifted behind him. He fell back, and a let out a sharp cry.

That's not possible. I put my back to the wall when I scooted in. Unless....

He remembered the cave-in. Maybe it had been hiding something all along. He reached around and felt nothing at his back. A soft pitter-patter startled him, and he rounded to see a flash of white melt into shadow behind him.

There can't be anything alive in here! It was hardly big enough for me to lie down flat.

He moved deeper into the mound—deeper than it should have gone, deeper than it ever had before. Step after step, his bewilderment grew, but so did his curiosity. The tunnel shrank smaller and smaller, forcing him first into a crouch, then a crawl. Only blackness lay in front of him and only silence behind, but the familiar brown velvet of earth still padded his hands and knees with its clammy cushion.

I should go back for a candle. If there is anything to see, it won't be very interesting in the dark!

But mother would never let him take a candle, and this tunnel didn't even exist last week.

What if it isn't here when I come back?

So, he pushed on. His crawl became a shuffle as the tunnel constricted even more, and he nearly turned back, but he found the dread of not knowing far outweighed his fear of going on.

Another rustle sounded in front of him.

I'll probably get eaten, and no one will ever know what happened to me.

The thrill of adventure sent a shiver up his spine and goosebumps down his arms. It urged him on. He put his hand out once more and found only dirt.

But I just heard something further on! This can't be the end.

He continued his blind investigation, moving his hand methodically across, up, then across again, careful to cover every inch. When his hand reached the level of his eyes, he felt an opening. Though surprised to find it angled up, he pulled himself into it and began to climb.

He continued up and up into darkness until he felt another wall of dirt. He pushed against it tentatively, startled when he broke through with almost no effort at all, revealing a shockingly bright light. Something shoved him from behind as if with invisible hands.

CHAPTER TWO

Normality is a paved road. It's comfortable to walk, but no flowers grow on it.

—Vincent van Gogh

Vincent released a ragged cry then closed his mouth in silent wonder. A new world lay before him. He rubbed his eyes.

I'm hallucinating. Or I've fallen asleep, and I'm dreaming.

He shook his head.

I suppose I could've crawled clear under the brook and right into Belgium….

But he knew he couldn't have gone as far as that because he'd accidentally wandered into Belgium once before, though, of course, not by means of traveling underground.

And this is nothing like Belgium anyway!

Red and orange leaves lit up the tops of the trees, brighter than any autumnal shade. Tall and willowy, they swayed in the breeze as if they lived in the water rather than the air. Long vines cascaded all around him, drifting this way and that, their blue-green buds fluttering and swirling around him like a thousand butterflies.

"It's Vincent, yes?"

Vincent jumped and spun, tripping over his feet and falling hard into a sitting position. But only a small white rabbit stared at him with its beady eyes. It sat unnaturally still—its nose didn't even twitch—and it only had one ear.

And then the rabbit opened its mouth and spoke. "Welcome to...."

Vincent screamed and scrambled to his feet.

"Don't be afraid," it said.

"But you're...you're a rabbit!"

"Yes, yes, something like that. Are rabbits alarming then? I really thought I'd picked the least threatening thing possible, but perhaps I chose unwisely."

Vincent stared in disbelief.

"I could change again, if you like," the rabbit said. "Would you rather I were bigger? Smaller? Looked something more like you?"

"You..."—Vincent stammered—"I don't even understand what you're saying."

"Don't you? I took great pains with the language, if nothing else."

"No, no. I understand the words perfectly. I just don't know what you mean."

The rabbit cocked its head. "Difficult distinction. Words are their meanings, aren't they?"

"I suppose. But are you saying you can turn into something else?"

"Yes, of course. I always forget how difficult this is," it muttered. "I haven't delivered a message in ages. I do try not to alarm the bodied creatures. It generally takes forever just to calm them down, but you're already listening, at least. The young ones are generally quicker. This isn't really my body as I haven't got one; I picked this form in order to communicate with you. This rabbit's body was sturdy and quick enough, but it's so much smaller than yours, it seemed harmless."

"You don't have a body?" Vincent asked.

"Not so to speak."

"Then what are you?"

"A herald."

"No, I mean, what do you look like if this isn't your body?" A flutter of leaves drew Vincent's eye. "And where are we?"

"Ah, yes, that second bit would be part of my communiqué, wouldn't it?" The rabbit stood on his hind legs, and a scroll of parchment materialized in his hands. He pulled a tattered string tied around the brown paper, unrolled the document, and began to read. "Vincent Willem van Gogh, welcome to Sian, this new world and so on and so forth, various formalities…." The rabbit's paw followed several lines of text before he spoke again. He seemed to be skipping over an awful lot of it. "Yes, here's the important bit: your skills are much desired to aid in the prevention of the severest of calamities. We know we can count on you, et cetera..."—he skipped some more—"...thank you for your kind attention. Please be advised as to the risks concerning bodily harm and/or bodily alteration of which all potentialities should be considered, including the possible cessation of your corporeal existence."

"That's terribly vague." Vincent attempted to peek around to read the letter himself, but the rabbit released the end of the parchment, and it curled up with a snap. "Do all the messages go like this? And do people often say yes without any further information?"

"Not as often as I'd like," the rabbit said, "but then as I told you, I don't bring very many messages."

"Well..." Vincent said, half to himself, "...if I could help prevent severe calamity in any world, I'd like to think I would try, notwithstanding the risk." He stared at the ground for a moment. "Are people in danger?"

"Certainly," the rabbit said. "This people will, in all likelihood, never exist at all if the danger is not thwarted."

"So, you're saying I'd be protecting this world's—Sian's—future?"

"Unquestionably."

"Why me?" Vincent asked. "I haven't really got any skills. I'm mostly a disappointment according to anyone you might ask."

"Well, then, let's not bother asking them," the rabbit said. "Going by all the wrong criteria, I'll wager. I seem to remember that being a common problem among the humans." Its nose twitched in a rabbit-like manner for the first time. "You know, I do think people usually ask more questions about the 'new worlds' bit."

Vincent shrugged and looked around. "I see worlds everywhere. This one's just bigger."

"Hmm…." the rabbit said. "I begin to understand why you were chosen."

"You haven't answered my question, though," Vincent said.

"Haven't I?"

"No," Vincent said. "Why me?"

"You will discover that in time." The rabbit waved dismissively.

"And you never told me what you really look like since this isn't your real body."

"Ah, that would take too long to explain, wouldn't it?" A pocket watch appeared in the rabbit's hand, and the he tapped its face impatiently. "Now, you must choose. We're late."

Vincent realized the letter seemed to have disappeared.

Wish I could've read all the parts he left out.

"Aren't you going to give me any more information?" Vincent asked. "Any idea what the disaster is? What my skill is?"

"That's all for now. More later, and you'll have another opportunity to return if you choose. Or I can take you back straightaway. Send you right back the way you came."

This jarred Vincent from his contrary line of questioning. "Oh, no. This is…." He trailed off, noticing once again the gentle vines swimming in the breeze, the magical quality of the light in the air. "This is a world worth saving, I think."

"Very well. We'd best be off then." The rabbit hopped a few paces, and Vincent fell to walking beside him.

"I'm not afraid of rabbits," Vincent said.

"But you were afraid of me?"

"Rabbits don't normally talk."

"Ah, yes. I suppose that might be discomfiting."

"And…umm…"—Vincent smiled a little—"you're missing an ear. Did you know? They have two."

"Oh, dear." The rabbit raised one paw to the side of its head. "Do they really? I only got a glimpse from the side, you know." He shrugged. "It's all the same to me. This is only for show anyway." He gestured to indicate his whole body.

Vincent wondered again what the rabbit's true form could possibly be but decided it would be useless to ask.

How can you be anything if you don't have a body?

Vincent lapsed into a long silence, drinking in the very essence of the place, comparing it to his own world. Its light was stronger, yet not harsher. Its air lighter, yet more substantial. Its earth wilder, yet more gentle. Vincent remained entranced by the vines wafting deftly in the breeze as if they weighed nothing at all. He felt lighter, too, as if he might be able to jump into the air and fly. The sun shone magnificently bright, catching in the translucent red and orange leaves and giving the impression of thousands of candles flickering overhead. Compared to this one, forests in his own world seemed thick and dark and heavy. He watched raptly as the light paled, casting a rosy hue over everything, passing into twilight and, finally, into the full dark of night. He'd been absorbing the newness around him, not wanting to sully it with talk, but as the darkness took over, a thousand questions formed in his mind.

By the time he spoke again, he followed the rabbit more by sound than sight. "What is your name, Rabbit?"

"Atralius."

"And where do we walk, Atralius?"

"On the terra of Sian."

Vincent laughed. "You're very literal, aren't you? I meant, where are we going? What are our ends?"

"That is an entirely different question."

The rabbit fell silent for several minutes before muttering, "Our ends…our ends…everyone bothering with the ends. Beginnings, too! Get far too much attention if you ask me. The middles are really the thing, you know. That's where everything happens, after all. What's the matter with them? Now, tell me, young Vincent: do you see the path before us?"

"Umm, no, actually. I can't really see anything at all. It's dark."

"Oh? Can you not? Well, my point exactly. There is no path. There often isn't. Not so as most people could tell, at any rate. We just keep on and eventually we come to the end, but if we can't enjoy the way until we get there, it's hardly worth going on. Now, let's find our friend."

"What friend?" Vincent said, a hint of fear creeping into his voice. The idea of meeting someone in the dark in a strange world sent a shiver down his back.

Atralius ignored this question altogether. "Mind you, she thinks she's finding us."

Footsteps approached in the dark.

CHAPTER THREE

What would life be if we had no courage to attempt anything?

—Vincent van Gogh

"Hello, my dear," the rabbit called out.

"Oh!" A cry came from behind them. "Who's there?"

"Why, don't you know, Mary Ann? You followed me nearly half the day."

"You're the rabbit, then?" she asked.

"That's what I've been told," Atralius said.

Vincent tried to think of a way to introduce himself so as not to frighten her, but the darkness made it terribly awkward.

The rabbit spoke again. "We've only just begun to look for you."

"Look for me?" she said. "But I was looking for you!"

"Yes, and you've found us! How delightful!"

"Did you say 'we' and 'us'?" A tiny quiver trembled in her voice. "Who else is here?"

"I am," Vincent said. "I'm Vincent. I suppose you're Mary Ann?"

"No, actually, I'm not. I'm Alice." She paused. "Were you expecting someone else?"

"I wasn't expecting anyone at all," Vincent said. "Atralius?"

"Oh," Alice said, "who's Atralius? Is someone else here, too?"

"No, that's the rabbit's name," Vincent answered.

"That's good, anyway." She sounded relieved. "I was beginning to feel a bit outnumbered."

Atralius spoke up. "I expected no one but you, Mary Ann. You're certain that's not your name?"

"Quite!"

"Interesting," the rabbit remarked.

A flutter filled the air, as of someone thumbing through a pile of pages.

"What are you doing, Atralius?" Vincent asked.

"Just checking my notes."

"But it's dark. You can't possibly see…."

"No," Atralius interrupted. "*You* can't possibly see, or so you say. I can see just fine. How about you, Mary Ann?"

"I can't see a thing, I'm sure!"

"Hmph." Atralius grunted, the sound of shuffling papers continuing all the while. "So limiting, your bodies. Glad I don't have one."

"What?" Alice said.

Vincent heard another little quaver in her voice. "Don't mind him. He's a rabbit as far as we're concerned."

"Oh, good. It is bothersome not being able to see you." She drew in a breath. "If he's a rabbit, Vincent, then what are you?" She had mastered the tremor in her voice but still didn't sound quite at ease.

"Oh, I'm a human," he said, a flutter of fear surfacing in his own mind. He managed to stutter a question. "And…uh…umm…you?"

"I'm a human, too," she said with a nervous chuckle. "I'm so glad you are."

"Aha!" Atralius cried out. "Someone's revised the notes! No one told me to expect a new version. Mary Ann is, apparently, averse to getting dirty, and that has overcome her curiosity."

"What has that got to do with anything?" Vincent asked.

"This one's come in her place, obviously." He crinkled some more papers. "You won't mind if I call you Mary Ann, dear? I memorized my notes millennia ago, and I'm not sure I can adjust."

"I…" she started.

"Good," Atralius said. "That's settled then. Now, I have a letter for you as well." He began reading. "Alice Pleasance Liddell…"

Vincent stopped him. "Is this going to be just like my letter?"

"Exactly so," the rabbit said.

"Then I think I can speed this up."

"By all means."

"OK, Alice," Vincent said, "this is a new world—it's called Sian, by the way— and it's in some kind of danger, and you and I have some skill required to prevent the disaster, but we're likely to die along the way. I asked a few questions that got me not much further than that, though I did establish we'd be protecting a future people who don't exist yet."

"Oh, I see," Alice said somberly. "Protecting yourself would be difficult if you don't exist yet. So, you've decided to continue on, Vincent?"

"Yes, but I'm sure you don't have to if you don't feel it's the right thing. I've always hoped I would be brave if given the responsibility." He paused. "And honestly, our world seems awfully dull after seeing just a bit of the beauty in this one. Atralius said we'd have another chance to change our minds, and no matter what, I don't like the idea of going back just yet."

"Yes," she said. "I quite agree."

"Wonderful!" Atralius said. "Now, let us march on."

The sound of his hops told them he'd already raced ahead, and they followed him as well as they could in the dark.

Suddenly, Vincent's foot caught on something, and he toppled forward, banging his knee when he landed.

"OW!" he cried, rolling over to regain his footing almost immediately.

"Are you OK?" Alice asked, concern spilling into her voice.

"Yes, just a bruise, I think," Vincent said, glad the darkness hid his face, which was surely reddening.

They'd fallen behind, and the rabbit's tiny footfalls pattered lightly as he backtracked. "Are you coming?"

"Yes, we're right behind you." Vincent brushed off his trousers and didn't mention the fall.

Several slight thumps told him Atralius had already bounded ahead.

"Vincent," Alice said, "I hope you won't think me forward, but would you hold my hand? I'm a bit afraid of falling, too, and it would be comforting to know where something—someone—is in this dark."

"Of course." His face grew even hotter. "I'm sorry I didn't offer." Alice's hand in his own calmed him somehow. "The dark doesn't seem quite as complete now. It's almost as if someone turned on a light."

"Is it?" Alice said. "I'm glad. I feel the same—as if I could never get lost now that you're holding my hand, and I don't even know where we're going!"

Vincent grew certain his face flushed brighter than his hair and remained infinitely grateful for the darkness.

"So, where are you from?" Alice asked.

"Zundert. What about you?"

"Zundert…." She sounded puzzled. "Is that on the coast beyond Bristol?"

"Bristol! No, it's in the Netherlands."

"The Netherlands?" Alice cried. "But your English is incredible. You haven't even an accent!"

"English?" he said. "I'm not speaking English, and neither are you."

"But I am. I only *can* speak English…well, and a very little French."

Atralius called back from ahead. "You'll not soon resolve this discussion. We're none of us speaking English."

"But, of course, we are." Alice said. "If English is the only language I know, then it logically follows that's what we're speaking."

"Logic has its faults, my dear, and when you followed a talking rabbit through your garden, you set it aside quite willingly."

"If we're not speaking English, then what are we speaking?" she asked.

"We're speaking human."

"And just what does that mean?"

Alice sounded indignant.

"It's a master language, like a master key. Every race has one, you know. If you could merge all the dialects from your world, you would come out with the human language."

"Why, that's absurd!" Alice said. "I've never heard of such a thing."

"You wouldn't have, would you? The master language is locked in your own world now. Only works if you're outside of it."

"Nonsense," Alice said. "That's like saying the master key only works if you're in someone else's house."

"That's about the size of it."

"A very impractical language then, if you…" she began.

But the rabbit interrupted again. "Finding it useful right now, aren't you, Mary Ann?"

"Oh!" Alice said, the little jerk of her hand telling Vincent she'd stamped her foot.

He grinned. "I think some conversations are pointless with our rabbit friend."

"Indeed," Alice said, "I think he's a bit mad."

Vincent laughed. "I'm not sure there's anything wrong with that. I like him better than many of the sanest people I know."

Alice giggled. "They are often boring, aren't they? Still, if he's going to call me Mary Ann, I'll just call him 'rabbit' as I have been doing in my head all day. It's not good manners, you know, to go on calling people by the wrong name once you know better."

"I quite agree." He grinned, despite Alice's annoyance. "So, how did you get here, anyway?" he asked, partly to change the subject and partly because he really wanted to know.

"My sister was reading a history book aloud, and it was frightfully boring. That silly white rabbit hopped across my lawn, and I didn't think a thing of it at first, but then he spoke! I'd never forgive myself if I didn't even attempt to investigate a talking rabbit, so I followed him through a hole and then somehow lost him before I came out the other side. I got awfully dirty, too; I quite understand Mary Ann's decision if she was to come the same way I did. It rained yesterday, and the tunnel was almost nothing but mud. I'm afraid my frock is in a shameful state."

Vincent laughed. "I'm probably no better. My story is nearly the same...only I was run...." He stopped, suddenly embarrassed to mention running from the town boys. "I climbed in a barrow mound on the moor and suddenly found the back was gone. There was a tunnel I'd never seen before, and a white blur vanished down it. I know now it was the rabbit, but I couldn't have said so at the time."

"A barrow mound?" Alice said, and Vincent felt her shudder. "Weren't you afraid?"

"No, I searched it ages ago and never found bones. That's how I knew the tunnel wasn't there before. I'd have never guessed it was a rabbit hole, though. Too big."

"But he's not really a rabbit, though, is he?" she said. "No matter what you said to make me feel better about it."

"No," Vincent said. "I don't think he's a rabbit at all."

CHAPTER FOUR

Admire as much as you can. Most people do not admire enough.

—Vincent van Gogh

"We're nearly there," Atralius called back after a few more minutes wandering in the dark.

"Good," Alice said.

"Indeed," Vincent agreed. "And I hope there are lights wherever we're stopping."

"And tea," Alice said. "And cakes. I'm starving."

"Here we are!" the rabbit said.

Something trailed across Vincent's face, and he nearly cried out but managed to keep it in.

Just vines.

He took another step, and his head slammed into something solid. "Ow!"

"Are you all right, Vincent?" Alice asked.

"Yes, but you might want to duck." He heard her gasp as she followed behind him. "You didn't hit your head, too, did you?"

"No, but it felt like a hundred spiders scuttled across my face." She shivered. "I don't like spiders."

"I think it's just vines."

"I do hope so."

Atralius seemed to be bustling around in the dark. "Now, Mary Ann, I need you to—"

"I beg your pardon," she interrupted. "This may be very rude of me, but I'm not sure I can stand the dark any longer. Haven't you a candle or an oil lamp…or…or…maybe a fire?" She whispered to Vincent, "I feel there are spiders all over me, and I'm sure I won't get over it until I can see."

"Certainly," the rabbit said, and a glow like a firelight banished the dark.

Alice smiled. "That's better!"

Vincent released her hand, suddenly very self-conscious to be holding it.

She looked back at the opening, brushing imaginary spiders from her hair. "Oh, vines, indeed. Thank goodness!" She turned to Vincent, and they stared at one another. Her long, dark hair lay untidily around her face, and she'd been right about her dress. Mud splattered nearly every inch of it. He inspected his own clothes. They were no better.

She laughed. "We are a pair, aren't we? But your hair is very exciting! It's just the color of fire!"

He combed the tangled curls with his fingers in a vain attempt to flatten it.

"Now, Vincent," she said, "I feel we know each other very well already, but we haven't been properly introduced, have we?" She curtsied. "How do you do?"

Vincent bowed stiffly and smiled as expected but wished they could've continued as before. He never liked the formalities. "I'm happy to make your acquaintance," he said and hoped Alice couldn't sense his displeasure.

Atralius seemed to be searching for something, and as he took no notice of them whatsoever, they took the opportunity to survey their surroundings.

"Why, we've stepped into an enormous tree, Vincent!"

"Yes." He touched the rough wood wall, and examined the contents of the rabbit's den, though his eyes kept drifting back to Alice. A squat brown cabinet small enough to belong in a child's play kitchen stood on one end with a dressing screen beside it, then a steamer trunk, then a low table with trays of tea and cakes on it.

"Oh, good!" Alice headed for the platters. "I am starving!" But she frowned and stopped, hand outstretched to pick up a cake. "Vincent, where is the light coming from?"

"I'm sure Atralius lit a lamp or…." He took a moment to check. No obvious source of illumination presented itself—no candle, no lamp, no fire.

Alice's voice interrupted his thoughts. "Atralius, where is the light coming from?"

"Why, I made it, obviously."

"Do you mean you just created it out of nothing?" Vincent asked.

"Certainly not. You can't make something out of nothing. But I need no tools to do so if that's what you mean."

"So," Alice said, "you could've lit our way the whole time instead of letting us stumble about in the dark?"

"Yes, of course, I could. Would you have preferred it?"

"Yes!" Alice and Vincent said in unison.

Alice laughed. "We told you we couldn't see!"

"Yes, but you didn't say you didn't like it," Atralius answered. He still puttered around the room, giving them no clues as to his aim.

Vincent laughed, too. "He is right, I suppose."

"Yes, we must be very definite with our preferences from now on," Alice said, "though I did find it pleasant to meet someone in the dark and get to know them before I'd ever seen them. If I could choose how to meet new people in the future, I should always want to do it in the dark, though I can't think how I'd arrange it." She reached for the tea cake once again. "Back to this then."

As Vincent, joined her, she pointed at the platters. A prettily drawn note stood on the tea tray like a tent. "Drink," it said. A corresponding one on the cake plate read, "Bite."

"How curious!" she said. "Why would one label them so, as if we needed directions?"

Vincent shrugged. "Shall we, then?" he asked, picking up the kettle.

"Indeed!" Alice raised her tea cake as if in a toast. "As instructed." She took a bite.

Vincent busied himself with preparing a cup of tea. "I suppose cold tea is better than none."

"Yes." Alice grimaced. "These aren't exactly satisfactory, either. Dry as dust." She coughed, then let out an odd gulp and dropped the remainder of her cake on the ground.

"What is it?" Vincent asked.

"I think…" she ventured, "…or at least, I thought…." She closed her eyes and touched the wooden wall beside her. "Vincent—I am—oh, I'm growing!"

CHAPTER FIVE

Do not quench your inspiration and your imagination.

—Vincent van Gogh

"Atralius!" Vincent shouted, his voice echoing in the tiny den.

The rabbit turned around indifferently. "Yes?" His eyes landed on Alice. "Oh, dear, what have you done?" He hopped across the room. "Didn't you read the labels?"

Alice wailed. "What is happening to me?"

Her head struck the roof, and her neck crooked at an alarming angle as she shot up and up faster and faster. She fell to her knees with a grunt, toppling the platter of cakes with a crash.

Vincent only just managed to move the tea tray in time to keep her from overturning that as well. The sound of fabric ripping reached his ears, and he averted his eyes, growing very afraid it was Alice's dress, which surely couldn't resist so drastic a growth spurt.

"Hand her the tea, Vincent."

But Vincent stood frozen, overwhelmed.

"Quickly, boy!" Atralius said.

Vincent still stared at the wall but held the cup over his head.

Alice did not take it immediately.

"Take it, Mary Ann!" the rabbit shouted. "And sip, don't guzzle!"

She presently obeyed. Taking the cup from Vincent, she took first one sip, then another.

Vincent couldn't help watching what happened now, and relief flooded him as her growth slowed, came to a halt, then, amazingly, reversed. If her dress had ripped, he couldn't tell. The front seemed perfectly in order.

Atralius reached for the cup and took it from her. "No more, no more. That should do."

Alice continued to shrink until she stood only just taller than Vincent.

"Good?" Atralius asked.

"I think," Alice said between hitching breaths, "maybe a little more."

He handed her the cup. "One more sip then."

Alice took another drink, sighed heavily, and handed the cup to Vincent with a trembling hand. "May I sit down?"

"Of course," the rabbit said, and a chair appeared out of nowhere.

She fell into it heavily.

Vincent rounded on the rabbit. "You might have warned us."

"I labeled them carefully. I'm sure it's not my fault."

Vincent leaned down to look at one of the notes now lying on the floor.

He picked it up and flipped it over. "Bite" on one side, "Height" on the other. He grinned and handed it to Alice.

"Well!" she said. "I never thought to look on the other side, and I wouldn't have known what it meant if I had!"

Vincent picked up the card on the tea tray and read this one aloud. "Drink." He flipped it. "Shrink." He laughed.

"I even made it rhyme in human, so you wouldn't forget," the rabbit said. "Not easy, you know, when it isn't your first language."

Alice laughed, too, and she and Vincent were both insensible for several minutes.

"Well,"—Alice finally caught her breath—"at any rate, I shall need a new dress." She reached a hand around to her back. "I'm afraid this one will no longer do." She wiggled her toes, now visible through the gaping holes in her shoes. "Nor these."

"I've just the thing," Atralius said. "But first...." He hopped over to one of the cakes and nibbled a bit.

"Is that a good idea?" Vincent asked.

"Yes." The rabbit took another bite. "Unlike some people, I know what I'm doing, and I'm finding this size rather inconvenient." He stood on his hind legs and grew slowly, till his head reached the height of Alice's shoulder. "Bit more then." He stopped just beyond Vincent's own height.

"Very good." He nodded, and his solitary ear flopped forward momentarily.

His longer legs changed his walk into an unusual, bouncy gait—something between a hop, a walk, and a shuffle. He pulled something from the trunk and handed it to Alice.

She took it and inspected it carefully, pulling it this way and that. "It's sort of like trousers and sort of like a dress, and it stretches just like taffy! I can't imagine what it's made of."

"Doesn't matter," Atralius said. "What matters is what it's made for. It will suit our purposes quite well." He tittered a laugh for the first time since their meeting. "'Suit…'" he said. "Ha! A suit that suits our purposes…I think I'm getting the hang of this language!"

Vincent and Alice exchanged glances, and Vincent whispered, "Perhaps so, but I'm not sure he's got the hang of jokes." They both burst into laughter again.

Alice stood and backed her way over to the dressing screen.

She reemerged moments later, and Vincent grew very silent. The tawny yellow of the dress set off her dark hair and reflected gold flecks in her amber eyes.

"I've never worn anything so comfortable!" She twirled in a circle, the skirt billowing like a wave. "I shan't mind growing and shrinking at all while wearing it." She hesitated and turned a wary gaze to the ceiling. "As long as we do it out of doors, at any rate."

"Now, Vincent," the rabbit said, "you'll get your own new clothes soon enough, but I gather from this debacle that the two of you may need some nourishment."

"Yes, please." Vincent nodded.

"If it wouldn't be a bother," Alice added.

Atralius twitched his nose and walked away muttering, "Bodies…so remarkably inconvenient with all their eating and drinking and seeing."

He ambled across the room and pulled a tray of bread and butter out of the cabinet. A teapot and two cups appeared next, and he began pouring.

"Why, it's steaming!" Alice remarked. "How did you heat it so quickly?"

"Heated it earlier to save time heating it now."

A dubious expression crossed Alice's face. "That's impossible."

"I assure you, it isn't," Atralius said. "How many impossible things have happened to you since breakfast this morning?"

Vincent grinned at her. "He has a point."

Alice raised the hand not holding the teacup and silently counted on her fingers. "I suppose you're right. I can think of as many as six off the top of my head." She shrugged and put the cup to her mouth but lowered it before taking a sip. "You're sure *this* tea is all right?"

"Perfectly normal," the rabbit said. "Regular as rain."

They polished off everything provided, down to the last crumb.

"If you're both finished," the rabbit said, "may we get on with our work?"

Alice nodded. "I'm ready for anything now I've eaten."

"Good. You, Mary Ann, will please search for your gloves. They are white, and I'm sure you won't mistake them."

"Pardon me," she said, "don't you mean your gloves?"

"No, why would I need gloves? I haven't even a body—not a real one, anyway."

"But I haven't any gloves with me."

"Ah, but you will when you find them," the rabbit said and moved on with no more explanation. "Vincent, you have need of a blindfold."

"I do?"

"Yes, I assure you that you cannot do without it."

Vincent shrugged, and they both began searching the room.

Several minutes passed, and Vincent still hadn't come across anything resembling a blindfold. Cupboards banged, and trunk lids creaked as Vincent hunted in every nook and cranny. He even looked inside the teapots.

There's only so many places to search!

Alice finally sighed. "Rabbit, must I have the gloves? I don't even want them, and if that's what you were hunting for this whole time and didn't find them, I'm sure I shan't either."

"Not true," Atralius said. "I haven't the knack for finding things amongst all these…things." He seemed to throw away the last word with a flick of his paw. "Not accustomed to it, you know. I'm sure you'll find them straightaway."

She looked at Vincent. "You can't find your blinder either?"

"No, and it's not a large room. If we haven't found them yet, it does seem unlikely."

"I'm not sure you're engaging all your efforts, though," the rabbit said.

Alice stiffened. "You shouldn't make personal remarks like that. It's very rude. You can see us searching, and you looked for twice as long without finding them."

"Well," Atralius said, "perhaps we'll do with a story instead."

"What does a story have to do with anything?" Vincent asked.

Alice closed the trunk and sat down on its lid. "It does seem a bit off our purpose."

"How do you know?" said the rabbit. "You've no idea what the story's about."

"I suppose that's true." Alice turned to Vincent. "Shall we sit at his feet just like little children listening to a bedtime story?"

"On the contrary," Atralius said, "the two of you are to tell the story to me."

"That's even less sensible!" Vincent said.

"Not at all! Telling a story you don't know will almost always help you find your way. I think you should begin, Vincent."

"But I don't know where to start!"

"Begin at the beginning," the rabbit said, "and go on till you come to the end; then stop. You and Mary Ann can take turns."

Vincent sighed. "If you say so." He sat down beside Alice and took a deep breath.

"There once were two children of about the age of twelve." He glanced sidelong at Alice hoping she wouldn't correct him, as if she could possibly know he were really only eleven. Her eager face encouraged him, so he went on. "They lived very regular lives during which nothing much happened at all. They learned reading and writing and sat for visitors and went on walks and were expected to behave quite respectably. Then one day, they saw something they could not ignore. Something unusual. They followed it into the dark and the dirt, knowing it may be foolhardy but not wanting to turn back."

He stopped and nodded at Alice who took up the tale.

"When they reached the end of the dark and the dirt," she said, "they burst out into a new world—one they could never have imagined. One of which sensible people would definitely not approve, because sensible people only want sensible things, and this world was anything but that. It was filled with wonder and nonsense and impossible things that made it shine in a way their own world never did."

She paused. "You go again, Vincent."

He nervously rubbed his hands along his knees. "They found they could grow and shrink by cakes and tea. They found lights that shone from nothing and a rabbit who talked and tea that heated itself." He stole a look at Alice. "And they held hands to keep from stumbling in the dark."

She smiled and put her hand on his.

He kept on. "And then the dark lifted a little...."

Alice suddenly interrupted him rather than being handed the story. "...because when they held hands, something happened—something small and very dim at first, but it grew more and more powerful as they went along. They could do things in this world they couldn't at home. They could speak a language they never knew existed and...and...find things that were hidden!"

Alice hopped up, pulling Vincent with her.

"Very good!" Atralius clapped.

"Shall we look again, Vincent?" she asked.

CHAPTER SIX

What color is in a picture, enthusiasm is in life.

—Vincent van Gogh

Vincent eyed Alice doubtfully. "I suppose, but…"

"Just trust me," she interrupted. "Don't you feel it?" She took his hand between both of hers. "We both did out in the dark, but we thought it was only comfort from having someone to hold on to. But just now, when I put my hand on yours…it's different. It's stronger now."

Vincent stared at her and nodded uncertainly.

"Let's find your blindfold first." She opened the trunk, shut her eyes, and reached her hand in.

Vincent watched as she moved a few items, never peeking, touching each for less than a second, then she closed her fist upon one. She pulled it out and handed it to him.

A long strip of navy cloth draped across her hand, its velvety sheen as smooth as the night sky, the silver edges sparkling like stars. He took it in his free hand. "But I looked in there!"

"I know!" Alice jumped up and down, never releasing Vincent's hand. "Isn't it exciting? It's like magic…oh!" She laughed. "I think it might *be* magic!"

She put her other hand on his shoulder. "You find the gloves, Vincent."

"But I don't know how!"

"Just try," Alice said, staring at him intently. "What comes to you naturally?"

He didn't answer and glanced over at the rabbit. Atralius was no help. He leaned against the wall with his arms crossed, watching them with a sly smile, saying nothing. Vincent felt his face getting hot. There might as well have been a hundred sets of eyes on him instead of just two.

Alice pressed, seemingly undeterred by his silence. "Just concentrate on what you want to find. Don't think about it, Vincent! Just do it!"

He wanted to crawl into a hole.

Then again, that's how I got here, isn't it?

He closed his eyes, retreated into his mind and pictured white gloves. He felt no closer to knowing where they might be and opened his eyes to find Alice's keen gaze had not left his face. He shrugged. "Am I just supposed to know where they are?"

"Oh, never mind. Maybe you can do something else! I'll do it." She closed her eyes and put her hand on the wall. She scrunched up her face. "It's this way, I think."

She pulled Vincent over to the small cabinet from which the rabbit had produced their bread and tea. She bent down and opened the lowest door. A grin spread wide across her face. She reached in and pulled out the gloves.

Alice squealed and hugged him indecorously. "We have magic powers, Vincent! I've never been so thrilled about anything. I wish I could tell Dinah—she's my cat, you know, and a very good listener." She rambled on. "But perhaps you have a different gift, Vincent. Mine definitely includes finding things, though I suppose we really know nothing about it! Perhaps we'll get more powers as we go along! It's much more noticeable when I'm holding your hand." She took one of his in her own again. "When we were telling the story and I put my hand on yours, I suddenly knew just where to look!"

Vincent glanced miserably at Atralius but faltered as the rabbit's edges wavered and blurred into his surroundings like a cloud dispersing in the wind. Vincent took a step back, releasing Alice's hand as he did so. The rabbit came back into focus immediately.

Vincent's chest heaved as he tried to regain his composure.

After all, I knew he hadn't a body.

Alice chattered on, apparently not noticing Vincent's alarm. She grabbed the rabbit's paw. "I believe you're a wizard! You fashioned that chair out of nothing and kept the tea hot in the cupboard and shone a light from nowhere!"

He delicately removed his paw from the overeager clasp of her hand. "Not a wizard…and you don't have magic powers, either. Just because you don't understand something doesn't mean it's magic. This world magnifies things. It's young, you see, and young worlds have so much more energy…just like children. And you can't help but absorb some of it, my dear, especially being young yourself. The gifts, though, those are yours—different in your own world, but still there. Vincent…"—he twirled a paw in the air as if introducing him to an audience—"has a talent for seeing things in ways other people can't…seeing, in fact, things the way they really are…a talent which he just discovered if I'm not mistaken. And you already had a knack for finding things, I'll warrant. The longer you're here, the stronger these gifts will become."

Vincent garnered his courage. "And why is it stronger if we hold hands?"

"Because you've given the energy somewhere to go." The rabbit drew a circle in the air with one finger. "When you hold hands, it goes into both of you, through both of you into the other, then back into the earth to make the circle again, building up stronger and stronger each time it goes around." He twirled his paw repeatedly.

"Like electricity!" Alice said. "Mr. Dodgson told me about it. It's a kind of power that likes to go 'round 'in a current,' he said. They're doing all sorts of experiments with it." She hesitated. "I don't really know what it's for, though."

"Yes, never mind," the rabbit said. "Irrelevant. So, now you know, and we can get down to business."

"Let me guess!" Alice bounced eagerly on her toes.

"How could you possibly guess?" Vincent asked.

"Well, logically, if my gift is finding things and your gift is seeing things other people can't, then certainly we must find something difficult to see." She shrugged. "It's obvious, isn't it?"

Vincent laughed. "You are a wonder, Alice."

"Oh, no." She grinned at him. "It's this place that's a wonder…a wonderland, actually. I shall always call it so." She paused. "But I'm right, aren't I, Rabbit? About finding something difficult to see?"

The side of the rabbit's face twitched, and Vincent grinned.

I think he's actually impressed!

"Yes, yes, very good," the rabbit remarked. "As I said, Sian is young, and there is a creature that searches for new worlds. It consumes time—the fresher the better. So, it follows that a fledgling world is an exotic buffet of the freshest delicacies for the Jabberwock—a veritable feast of new and unusual flavors."

"You speak of time as if it's an actual thing," Vincent said.

"A thing?" Atralius exclaimed. "Hardly! No, no, Time's a good friend of mine. So, you can imagine, he's not very fond of being eaten, any more than he is of walking backwards, which he only agrees to do on very special occasions."

Alice's eyes grew wide. "Do you mean something like...Father Time?"

"Well, you can call him 'father' if you like. I shan't. He's hardly older than I am."

"But how *can* he be eaten? How is he still alive?" Worry troubled her face like a ripple in a pond. "And what would happen if Father Time were dead?"

"Oh, there's enough of Time to keep a few nibbles from killing him, but he tells me it is very unpleasant. Makes him feel ragged. Time is really only ever borrowed, you know, so he's used to having all his bits back in the end. But when the Jabberwock indulges his appetite, the time is lost forever. Not to mention the creatures he steals it from. Dreadful for them since they have so very little time to begin with."

"What creatures?" Vincent asked.

"The ones the Jabberwock steals the time from, of course."

"I'm quite confused," Alice said. "I thought it was eating Father Time."

"Oh," the rabbit cried. "You don't imagine the Jabberwock has found Time himself, do you? We wouldn't even be here if he had. No, it's the pieces he's loaned out. Very unfortunate. It takes every bit of Time a creature possesses."

"So..." Alice said, "what happens to them?"

"They die, of course. In mere moments, they progress through the rest of their lives and shrivel away into corpses before your eyes. And he's fast, the Jabberwock.

He can age a troop in moments. If he has you in his grasp, it's too late." The rabbit clutched a fist in the air as if demonstrating. He shuddered. "Appalling to witness, I assure you."

Dread entered Vincent's gut.

If the rabbit's horrified, it must be truly awful.

Alice sat, chin resting in her hands, staring at the blank tree wall. "So, it only wants the new things, this Jabberwock? It won't eat us?"

"Oh," Atralius said, "I never said it wouldn't eat older things. It will eat anything if it's hungry enough...or if its provoked. And I wager you're young enough yet to tempt it a little."

Vincent's shock grew at this speech, but Alice went on matter-of-factly.

"So, the very newest things would be, to it, like a delicious plum pudding is to me, and something a little older might be like bread and butter, and the very oldest things would be like eating a carrot or something I'd really rather not, but will if I must?"

"I daresay that's the idea," Atralius said.

Vincent stared at her, stunned, then his laughter bubbled up until he could no longer contain himself. "Alice! I believe only you could make me laugh at this moment."

She laughed with him. "I'm only trying to understand it all."

"Yes, well, there's little cause for merriment." A hint of disapproval entered the rabbit's voice as he waved his arm in the air. Something like a floating window opened in the middle of the room.

Alice gasped, and Vincent gaped in wide-eyed disbelief.

"This may clear your heads," Atralius said. "You need to know what you're up against."

A picture swirled into the opening and when the things in the picture began to move, Alice cried out. The rabbit paid no attention whatsoever to their astonishment until Alice jumped up and ran to the other side of the impossible apparition. She passed her hand through it. "Why! There's nothing there!"

"Very shocking, I'm sure." Atralius took Alice's hand and led her to stand next to Vincent, shaking his head all the while. "The old ones are so frightened and the young ones so flighty!" he muttered. "Pay attention, will you? It's imperative you both see this."

They watched a story unfold through this magical window. A small creature not unlike a squirrel trundled about on the ground, digging here and there, little nose twitching.

"This is what should be—what was." Atralius waved his hand. "But this is what is."

The picture changed so quickly Vincent nearly missed it when he blinked. Only a tiny leathery body remained, dried and withered as if someone had lain it in the sun for many months.

"Oh!" Alice put a hand to her mouth. "The poor dear!"

The rabbit waved his hand again and the image faded from view. "This is what will happen to all of Sian's creatures—plant and animal—for to devour Time from the first fruits is the Jabberwock's most decadent craving. After that, it will take the youngest, for their Time is fresh and their stock nearly full. Then it will consume all in its path until the world falls silent in ruin, its life taken before it's rightly begun."

Vincent felt depleted.

"But do not despair, children," Atralius said. "If even one still stands against evil, there is hope." He walked across the den. "We also have this." He pulled a longsword from behind the cabinet, and a surge of courage suddenly filled Vincent's chest.

CHAPTER SEVEN

In the end, we shall have had enough of cynicism, skepticism, and humbug, and we shall want to live more musically.

—Vincent van Gogh

The blade shone, reflecting the golden light in shimmers like fireflies flitting about the room. Its hilt glinted with tiny jewels of red and amber, interweaving in a crisscross pattern below the grip.

Vincent gazed in awe. The sword alone would have fascinated him, but gleams of light emanated from it, gold and silver sparks darting all around it as if it were bursting with life.

He glanced up at Atralius who watched him intently.

"It is something, isn't it, Vincent?" Atralius held the sword out to him.

Vincent backed away shaking his head. "No, I…I couldn't." But his hands stretched out almost involuntarily, and he took it from Atralius. A jolt of energy ran through every muscle. "It's powerful, isn't it?"

"Can you see it, then?" the rabbit asked.

Vincent nodded timidly, the strangeness overwhelming him with nearly equal parts of wonder and fear. "And feel it, too." He ran his finger down the flat of the blade. "Do you see it, Alice?" He glanced up at her.

"Well, it's a lovely sword, of course." She studied him. "But you see more than that, don't you, Vincent?"

"A little," he said.

"I'm glad." She smiled.

"It is infused with light," Atralius said. "Real light, you know. And only a weapon infused with light can kill the Jabberwock."

"So, we do have to kill it?" Alice looked forlorn for the first time and slumped into the chair. "I suppose I knew we must."

"But why us?" Vincent asked. "We're just kids."

"That's no excuse," the rabbit said. "Youth often understands duty better than age, and you've already proven your gifts, so let's get to the point.

"Yes, how do we do it, Rabbit?" Alice straightened. "Tell us everything."

Vincent stared at the sword again but thought of Alice. She seemed to take the whole world in stride, whatever it threw at her.

Not like me.

He felt like an ocean with no control of his own waves, tossed about and confused, dangerous and afraid all at once. He glanced at her eager eyes.

I wish I could be like that. Daring, excited, unafraid of what may come....

"Vincent!" The rabbit's stern voice broke the spell. "Were you attending anything I just said?"

Vincent felt the heat rising in his cheeks.

Did she see me staring at her?

"Umm, no, sir. I was captivated by the...umm... sword, sir."

"Well, pay heed. Alice will catch you up on anything important you missed. The Jabberwock is like me in that it has no body. But unlike me, it has chosen a form so that it may indulge its appetites. It needs no food for sustenance but consumes all it can, nevertheless. It can't be seen until it takes its feeding form unless it wants to be. Any other time, it can appear as anything it wishes or not at all."

"So," Vincent said, "you're saying we might meet it and never know it was the Jabberwock?"

Alice interjected. "Or that it may be invisible altogether?"

"I'm afraid so," Atralius said. "But you, Alice, will be able to find it, and you, Vincent, will be able to see it, no matter its form as long as you're using your gifts. So, you'll be able to see it coming."

"What a comfort," Vincent said.

The rabbit began pacing. "Heed this or your efforts will be in vain." He stopped and locked eyes with each of them in turn. "It is only vulnerable in its feeding form. It is useless to attack until it takes this state. It must be on the verge of feeding." The rabbit's last words hung like punches in the air.

"But that means,"—Alice swallowed—"it'll be on the verge of killing someone."

"Yes," the rabbit said, "but you'll be ready, won't you?"

"Oh, dear," Alice said.

Atralius turned to Vincent. "What do you see when you look at the sword?"

The blade lay across Vincent's lap. He trailed his fingers across the jewel-encrusted hilt. "It's sort of faint, but it seems to radiate life and light and power. The colors all swirl together in patterns like smoke from a fire and then fade away the further they get from the sword."

The rabbit nodded.

"Yes, and the Jabberwock's form will do the opposite. It will drain colors into its darkness and extinguish their light. Whatever you do, you must give the monster a mortal wound. A scratch will not do, nor a stab in the leg." He continued pacing. "Aim for the heart,"—he thrust with an imaginary sword—"or the head,"—he held his fencer's stance—"and if at all possible, take its head off altogether!" He startled them with a sudden slash in the air, and Vincent felt the whoosh of the wind as the rabbit's arm passed above his head.

"But that's horrid!" Alice said.

"Better than having all your years stolen in a flash," the rabbit said tersely.

Neither of them argued with that.

Atralius took the sword from Vincent and leaned it next to the door.

"You may still choose to go back," he said, "now that you have the full picture."

Vincent remembered the speech he'd given in the dark when Alice asked if he'd chosen to go on.

Do I still want to be brave?

And he was surprised to find that he did. A quick glance revealed a gleam of resolve in Alice's eyes.

He faced Atralius. "What do we do next?"

"First, you must be fitted up, Vincent," he said. "Those clothes will never do for shrinking and growing."

The rabbit walked over to the trunk and began digging again. A moment later, he held up a pair of bright blue trousers and a white shirt with pearl buttons down the front. Next, he drew out a pair of navy shoes. "Anything in your pockets will grow or shrink with you, but you can't carry any packs. The resizing doesn't extend that far."

"Umm…" Vincent hesitated.

"Yes?" Atralius asked.

"The sword? It's not going to fit in anyone's pocket."

"Oh, it doesn't count. It's vorpal just like the clothes."

They gaped at him blankly.

"What?" the rabbit said.

"Vorpal?" Alice said. "We don't know what that means."

"Ah, yes. I forgot it doesn't translate into human. Humans don't have vorpal things. The best way I can describe it is it will assume the perfect size and then take that size appropriately."

"Wait." Vincent's eyes grew wide. "Are you saying that in some worlds, things routinely change sizes on their own?"

"Of course," the rabbit said. "As long as you're touching the sword when you change sizes, it will adjust accordingly. I'm sure you're very interested in what kinds of things there are in other worlds and how they all work, but there's no time for that."

"But think of it, Vincent!" Alice cried. "What if everything were vorpal! I should never have to alter another dress or do up a hem! And the trains would never be crowded!"

"To be sure," Atralius said. "Now, go change into your things, Vincent."

He thrust the garments into Vincent's hands and ushered him behind the screen just as Alice picked up her old dress.

"I'm glad you reminded us of pockets, Rabbit. I've a box of comfits I would have missed later. I believe candies will be a welcome treat on this sort of adventure!"

She had finished transferring them from her old frock by the time Vincent rejoined them in his new clothes.

Alice clapped her hands. "My, but you look dashing!"

He lowered his head shyly. "I feel a bit foolish."

"Not at all!" Alice took his hands, putting one of them on her waist and the other on her shoulder.

"We're fit for a ball!" She twirled him around, laughing.

The attention alone rendered Vincent nearly speechless, but his sight had grown stronger already, and when Alice touched his hands, the lights he'd seen wavering around her dimly before now flitted and flamed as bright as the sun. Crimson and burgundy trailed around her, setting her aglow. The colors washed the room in dances of their own, and he thought he may die from sheer wonder. Tears stung the backs of his eyes, and he made a show of ending the dance by bowing to Alice and releasing her to ease his vision.

It's beautiful, but...staggering. And this is to get stronger? How will I stand it?

"Atralius," he said, "you said our gifts will get stronger while we're here?"

"Yes, I'm fairly certain of it."

"And just how strong will they get?"

The rabbit turned to look at him. "Why, as strong as you let them, I'd think." He changed topics but kept talking. "You'll each need a supply of cakes and tea...."

"Wait," Vincent interrupted him. "You mean we control how strong they get?"

"Well, if you are very irresolute about them, it could result in some instability. That's how gifts usually are, you know. They're there, but if you don't commit to them, they're not worth very much."

Vincent would have continued the conversation, but the rabbit bustled about, apparently searching for the aforementioned cakes and tea. "Now, I recommend cakes in the right pocket. 'Bite, height, right,' you know. And then you'll put the tea in your left pocket and, unfortunately, that doesn't rhyme at all, but one can only do so much."

Alice giggled. "Fancy putting tea in our pockets!"

The rabbit's nose twitched terribly at that, whether in annoyance or amusement, Vincent couldn't tell.

"We'll put it in vials, of course," the rabbit noted. "So, 'drink; shrink.' Got it?"

They nodded, and Vincent decided to put worry from his mind.

"And don't eat it just because you're hungry. It's not for nourishment and will only make you hungrier no matter how much you take in."

"Will it?" Alice furrowed her brow. "What shall we eat then?"

"I daresay you'll find enough to eat in the forest."

"But mightn't we accidentally eat something poisonous?" she asked. "Many things are you know."

"The animals will help you discern."

"The animals?" Vincent said. "But how? Can they talk?"

"Under ordinary circumstances, no, but as you've need of guides, I've given a special dispensation. The intelligent species has yet to be created here, and the Jabberwock must be defeated before then or all will be lost."

"I've always wanted to talk to animals!" Alice said, not responding to the second part of this speech at all. "If only Dinah were here! I'm always wishing I could read her thoughts. She stares right into my eyes and listens so earnestly."

"Just some of the animals, mind you," the rabbit continued. "Only the ones who can help you on your way."

Alice let out a little cry. "Rabbit, is that why we need to shrink? To talk to the animals?"

"Yes. Or that's one of the reasons anyway. Can't go plodding up to them like giants and expect to make any progress. They're as likely to bite as to speak if you go around like that."

Alice grinned from ear to ear. "It's so exciting, isn't it, Vincent?"

Atralius continued running around the room arranging things and handing them items to put in their pockets, giving instructions all the while. He finally stopped and said, "All right then. Off you go."

"Right now?" Alice said.

"Well, why not?"

"It's the middle of the night!" As if to prove her point, she promptly yawned causing Vincent to do the same.

"Oh, bother, I've forgotten again. Those dratted bodies of yours. I suppose now you need a sleep?"

"I'm afraid I shall be no good at all without one," Alice said.

"Nor I." Vincent agreed.

The rabbit sighed. "All right, then." He flicked his paw and two cozy pallets materialized on the floor. "There you are. Alert me when you've finished."

Their pallets lay end to end, and they crawled into the piles of pillows and coverlets, putting their heads together in the middle.

"I didn't realize just how tired I was." Vincent yawned again, pulling a downy blanket up to his chin.

"Nor I," Alice said. "I can barely keep my eyes open. And these blankets are the loveliest things! It's just like I'm wrapped up inside a big, fluffy cloud."

"I know." Vincent glanced across the room. "Look at Atralius," he whispered.

She opened her eyes to peek. "Why, he's just standing there glaring at us!"

Vincent stifled a laugh, but Alice seemed quite put out. "I shall never sleep if he watches us that way all night." She sat up on her elbow. "Rabbit?"

"Yes," he said.

"Are you going to watch us like that all night?"

"Well, I've nothing else to do until you're on your way."

"It's impolite to stare, though."

"Is it?"

"I'm afraid so."

"As you wish then." He sat down in the chair facing the other direction. "Is this better?" he called over his shoulder.

"Much," Alice said. "Thank you."

She lay her head back, and in mere minutes, her deep breaths told Vincent she already slept.

He stayed awake much longer, thinking about his new vision. He glanced up at Alice, her dark hair falling in tendrils about the blanket.

I could test it.

He'd released Alice's hand so quickly before he'd only gotten a sort of impression.

I do want to know what Atralius really looks like. I get the feeling it might be worth seeing.

He reached up over his head tentatively, letting the merest tips of Alice's hair tickle the ends of his fingers.

Everything in his sight swirled and eddied as if in an ocean tide. He gazed above his head for a moment, taking it all in, the browns and yellows leaking from the walls in trails like smoke from a candle.

Now for Atralius....

CHAPTER EIGHT

I don't know anything with certainty, but seeing the stars makes me dream.

—Vincent van Gogh

Where the rabbit's head should have risen above the back of the chair, rapturous beauty such as Vincent had never imagined swirled and surged like a sunset speeding through an open sky. He drew in a sharp intake of breath.

He's like a star in the heavens! Only…all the colors!

The vortex of light and color rushed at such a great speed that Vincent could only bear it for a moment.

He pulled his fingers away from Alice's hair. The back of the rabbit's head returned, but a bit wavery as if this new sight would vanquish his old.

His heart thundered in his chest. He closed his eyes, the image still before him as if it were burned into his memory, and despite his weariness, he did not find it easy to fall asleep.

They woke early to the sounds of the rabbit clanging about conspicuously.

Vincent yawned.

Alice sat up and rubbed her eyes. "It wasn't a dream! I was awfully afraid I would wake up in my own boring bed." She jumped up without hesitation. "We are going to have breakfast first thing, aren't we? I'm famished."

"Yes, I've pulled out all the things for you." The rabbit waggled a hand in the direction of the food.

Vincent rose, raking fingers through his hair, certain it stuck out in every direction.

Alice poured them both cups of tea.

"Sugar and milk?" she asked as Vincent joined her.

He nodded blearily.

"I slept just like a baby, Vincent," Alice said. "I mean I slept the way they pretend babies sleep, not the way they really do with all that waking and wailing. The saying really ought to be 'I slept like a cat.' What about you?"

"Good, I think, though I'm not fully awake yet," he said.

"Oh, I am," Alice said. "I couldn't possibly stay sleepy with all this excitement floating about." She inhaled deeply and smiled at him with bright eyes.

Vincent smiled back and glanced at the sword leaning against the doorpost. A shiver of anticipation ran down his spine, but he couldn't shake a rising fear. Everything in the den wavered indistinctly, and he worried about what this meant. He glanced at the rabbit. Though a bit intimidated after his vision the night before, he had to ask.

"Atralius, will these gifts affect us even when we're not using them?"

"Well, as I said, they'll get stronger the longer you're here and the more they're practiced. So, I'd say it's possible they'd eventually become dominant and take over your natural state."

"And when we go back to our world?"

"Your world won't have the youth of this one to invigorate the gifts, so they'll be tamed, I think, but still in effect, yes."

"So, however strong this special sight becomes here, it's likely to be at least somewhat changed when I go home?"

"Yes, I'm fairly sure, though as I said, it will only become as strong as you let it."

That's what I was afraid of.

His new sight, however incredible and magical, transformed everything drastically. How would the water beetles look in this new sight with their shiny backs and the little ridges on their legs? And the birds with their delicate wisps of feather? And his mother's face with its stern mouth and creases around the eyes? He pictured the crisp lines of stalks grown tall all summer, swaying in the breeze as he stared across the creek. And then he thought of what he'd seen the night before—that melding of one thing into another and the rabbit's total transformation. What might things at home look like? And people?

Could I ever grow accustomed to it?

He ate in silence, attending to none of the conversation until they finished the meal and the rabbit grabbed him by the shoulders, pulled him to his feet, and shoved him toward the door.

"Now, you've got your cake in the right pocket and your tea in the left, yes?"

Vincent patted his pockets and nodded.

Atralius handed him the sword and a sling of sorts. "Strap on the scabbard. And keep it on you! Don't leave it lying about."

Vincent fiddled with it for several minutes, attempting, unsuccessfully, to buckle it around his waist. Alice came to his rescue.

"Here, let me." She took it from his hands. "This kind doesn't go around your waist. It's a back scabbard, so it crisscrosses like this."

"Well, that explains why I couldn't figure it out." He smiled. "How do you know so much?"

"There's lots of people practicing their fencing at Father's college." She grinned mischievously. "He doesn't like me to watch, but it's so exciting, I can't help it."

"Maybe you should take the sword then," Vincent said.

She arranged the straps across his shoulders and buckled it in front of his chest. "Oh, no. The rabbit gave it to you, and you'll be able to see the Jabberwock coming even if I don't know it's there."

"I suppose." Vincent sighed.

She pulled on the straps of the scabbard. "Now, how's that?"

He readjusted it across his back. "Perfect." He smiled at her. "Thank you." He turned to the rabbit who had begun clearing up the breakfast plates. "Do you have any more instructions for us, Atralius?"

"Only this:"—he stood from his task and held one finger in the air—"practice your gifts. They'll probably get stronger on their own, but the more you practice, the stronger they will be, and the stronger they are, the better your chances." He strode toward the door. "And if you have a chance to kill the Jabberwock, don't hesitate. You may not get another."

The rabbit shooed them out the leafy doorway. "No questions?" He didn't wait for an answer. "Good. I'm late already. Always late when dealing with bodies." He went back into the hollow tree, leaving them standing alone in the woods.

They stared at one another blankly, stunned a little by the rabbit's rushing.

"One more thing." Atralius's head popped back out. "Be decisive. Focused. Resolute!" He said this last word with excessive gusto, then added in a normal tone, "Remember that. Very important."

He retreated into the hollow tree again, and Alice laughed.

Vincent couldn't help but laugh with her. "You are the best person in the world to go on an adventure with, Alice. Half the people I know would have sat down and started crying on the spot ten times over, and we haven't even truly begun!"

"It's too fantastic to cry about!" She grinned, turning around to face the forest. "And now, I suppose we ought to decide which direction to go."

"That'll be you," Vincent said.

She nodded and walked to the nearest tree. She put her hand on it and closed her eyes, scrunching them up as if she were working out a very difficult sum. Only a moment passed before she opened them and pointed. "That way."

They started off with the birds chirruping their morning songs.

"How did you know to put your hand on a tree like that?" Vincent asked.

Alice shrugged. "It just felt right."

Vincent stopped mid-stride. "Atralius forgot something for all his preparations!"

"What is it?" Alice said.

"I haven't got my blindfold, and he made such a fuss about it, I guess we shouldn't go on without it."

"Oh, indeed!" Alice agreed. "I don't have my gloves, either!"

She hesitated upon reaching the opening into the rabbit's den. "Shall we knock or just walk right in?"

Vincent shrugged. "I've an idea Atralius wouldn't care at all."

She nodded and parted the leaves, calling out, "Rabbit!" She stepped within and gave a little cry.

Vincent hurried in behind her.

She spun, surveying the room. "It's all gone! Everything…is just gone."

CHAPTER NINE

I am always doing what I cannot do yet in order to learn how to do it.

—Vincent van Gogh

Alice pointed. "Everything except the blindfold and the gloves."

They lay neatly in the middle of the floor.

"I should be surprised," Vincent said, "but I'm not."

She handed the blindfold to Vincent and promptly put on her gloves, which reached all the way up to her elbows.

"Well,"—she stepped back out of the tree—"if he isn't a wizard, he's something. Don't you agree?"

"He's definitely something." Vincent thought of his vision.

"What do you suppose they're for, though?" Alice held her arms out and twisted them over, examining the gloves. "I don't feel any different."

Vincent shrugged. "He might've told us."

"No matter," Alice said. "We'll discover it along the way most likely. Let me check our direction and see if I can tell a difference. And you should put on the blindfold and see if anything happens."

She approached a tree and rested her hand on it.

"Anything?" Vincent asked.

"Yes." She furrowed her brow. "It's definitely less cloudy. You try your blindfold."

He took it from his pocket and wrapped it around his head.

Alice took the ends from him and tied it in the back. "Try to see something," she said.

"But what? It's pitch-black with this thing on."

"I don't know. Anything."

"This is silly." He raised one side of it to peer at her. "How am I supposed to see anything if I can't see anything?"

"Vincent!" Alice exclaimed. "How clever you are! What if that's just how it works? I find things by touch, but I'm not really using my hands, am I? You need to see things, but your real eyes couldn't possibly see the way you need to, could they? Shut them out, and maybe your special sight will take hold."

Vincent sighed and concentrated. He willed the sight into existence, visualizing Alice as she had been when they danced, little rivers of red and orange pirouetting around her.

And suddenly she stood before him just so, transformed—the shape of a girl going up in flames.

Only the fire is from the inside.

Vincent could not mistake Alice. Though indistinct in this altered sight, the swirl of motion captured her every expression more perfectly than he could have imagined.

…because it's the real Alice. I'd recognize her anywhere.

He looked around slowly, trying to take in the rest of the scene.

"You do see something, don't you, Vincent?" Alice clapped excitedly. "I knew you would!"

This new vision rendered him speechless. The liveliest of colors spiraled and whorled and imbued everything with its own subtle hue, a mesmerizing intermingling of light and form.

Alice touched his arm, and his sight intensified so dramatically, he flinched. The images raced before him, and he drew in a deep breath. He opened his mouth to speak but stopped. A black vine defaced the beauty—like a fowl smoke rising from a toxic fire. It tarnished the colors around it, reaching and grasping like a malicious hand.

Is it the monster?

He took off at a run, but toward it, not away. "Stay here, Alice!" he yelled back.

He neared the site, reaching across his shoulder to grab the sword, but then he saw the remnants. The source of the black lay before him—a small, withered body—some hapless creature devoured.

Not the Jabberwock, but its work.

"Vincent!" Alice yelled.

She approached behind him, crashing through the leaves, but stopped short when she saw what he was looking at.

As much as Vincent hated seeing the little corpse, watching Alice see it was worse. Her color paled into a chalky counterfeit of her natural brightness and flickered dangerously as if it may go out like a candle.

He tore off the blindfold, dropping it to the ground, and the phantasm of color dissipated. His normal sight already blurred even more than it had at breakfast. He shook his head, tried to ignore it, then looked back at the dead animal on the ground.

Alice sat down beside it, and Vincent joined her. He forgot about the sword, and it drove into the earth at his back, knocking him off-balance as he lowered himself to the ground.

Alice didn't seem to notice. "What kind of creature do you think this poor animal was, Vincent?"

"It's…." He paused and shook his head. "I'm not sure." He had almost said it was too shriveled to tell but had adjusted his words.

Tears trickled down Alice's cheeks, glistening like diamonds. "We have to stop it, Vincent."

He nodded, but a gnawing fear returned in his belly, and he couldn't rid his mind of the image of that withered creature. Blackness had curdled around it as if death itself lingered, ready to infect any who drew near. Whatever did this was evil—pure evil.

And this is just the mark it leaves behind.

They sat beside the little animal's body for some minutes, but he finally took a deep breath and put a hand on Alice's shoulder, grimacing as the touch enhanced his sight and a murky shadow wavered around the little corpse on the ground. "It's time we moved on, Alice."

She rose and walked away in silence.

Vincent picked up the blindfold, stuck it back in his pocket, and followed her. They strolled for some minutes before he thought to ask, "Alice, are we still going the right way?"

A puzzled expression troubled her face. "I...I don't know. I didn't even think of it. I can't stop thinking of that poor dear."

"Me, too. But let's test our direction."

She nodded and reached for the nearest tree. Her "seeking face" appeared, but her expression did not relax into a knowing smile as before. She opened her eyes. "I think it's this way."

"You think?"

"I'm pretty sure, anyway," she said.

Vincent nodded. "Good enough for me. Lead the way."

Many silent minutes passed, only their own dull footfalls thumping in the damp underbrush. The forest thinned out a little, and a gentle breeze reached them. The trees were shorter than those Vincent had seen upon arrival, their branches laden with seed pods the size of grapefruit. These dotted the ground as well, and Vincent began absentmindedly kicking one down the path ahead.

Alice stopped. "Let's play a game. Shall we, Vincent?"

"A game?"

"Yes. I'm still not quite over seeing that little creature. I'm a bit nervous, and I'm sure a game would help get our sense of adventure back." She nodded firmly. "You play croquet, yes?"

"Alice...." He started to protest.

"It'll only take a few minutes, Vincent." She had rightly guessed his thoughts. "I know we can't play a proper game." She smiled at him. "We need something to cheer us up, though. We can take turns being wickets, and we could use sticks for the mallets and these seed pods that fall from the trees—or whatever they are—for the balls. We're even in a nice sort of flat place for it. It'll be awfully inexact, but who cares?"

Vincent watched her with a mixture of annoyance and amusement. She gathered a few of the seed pods from the ground and made a pile of them in the center of the clearing.

She reached for a stick. "And this will make a perfect mallet."

He started toward her. "No, Alice, wait...."

But it was too late. The thing in her hand curled around her arm as fast as lightning, teeth snapping viciously.

She screamed and tried to drop it, but it held her now as opposed to the other way around.

"Get it off! Get it off!" She flailed her arms about madly.

"Stop moving!" Vincent yelled, trying vainly to catch hold of her arm. "I'll never get it off if you're waving about like that!"

She froze, eyes closed tight, and whimpered softly. "Oh, Vincent, what is it? I don't dare open my eyes. Is it horrid?"

"It's not that bad. It's kind of cute, actually." While she talked—which her fright hadn't stopped her from doing—he managed to grab it by the tail with one hand and just behind its head with the other. He slowly unwound it from her arm. "I've almost got it. Did it bite you?"

"I don't think so."

"OK." He pulled it from her arm. "Want to look before I let it go?"

She turned, a sort of squeamish fear on her face morphing into a sunny grin almost immediately. "How can I have thought it a stick? It's like a long, thin badger…or… or…a ferret!"

"Yes, more like a ferret," Vincent said, "only slithery."

"Look at its little face!" Alice ran a finger down its back. "I thought it was something like a snake with claws, but its fur is just terribly flat and shiny."

It bared its teeth at her, but she took no notice. "It's just as smooth as butter!"

It thrashed terribly in Vincent's hands.

"Yes," he grunted, "and just as difficult to hold. It's about to wriggle right out of my grasp."

"Don't let it go just yet." Alice reached into her pocket and pulled out the tin of comfits. "You'd like one of these, I'll wager."

"Alice, I can't hold it forever." Vincent bent his arms awkwardly to prevent it getting its head around so it could bite him. "We don't have to make friends with every creature we come across."

"Not every creature, Vincent," she said, "but I'm sure I've offended this one."

She held the candy near its face, and though its expression still menaced, its nose twitched in decided interest.

"I'm going to put this down, dear, and then Vincent will let you go so you can eat it."

The animal followed the comfit with its eyes.

"All right, Vincent. Put him just near it and back away."

Vincent was glad enough to give it some space. The creature wasn't large, but its teeth seemed daunting enough.

It scurried a few feet away then rounded to face them, hissing as it did so. Dark streaks ran down its back and faded into the mottled gray-brown of a shady forest floor.

"It does sort of look like a stick," Vincent conceded.

The creature's nose twitched, and it rooted in the dirt until it landed on the candy and gobbled it greedily.

It started to run away then its beady eyes darted back to Alice. She took a step nearer, and it backed away, lowering itself to the ground defensively.

"None of that, my dear. Don't be naughty." She put another comfit on the ground and took a step back.

It advanced and nearly swallowed it whole.

Alice leaned down. "There, are we friends now?"

It looked at her askance and skittered a few steps off.

"I think that's as friendly as it's going to get," Vincent said.

"Well, I love it. I do miss Dinah. I wish she could see it." She frowned. "Though I expect she'd only try to eat it. Better she's still at home, I suppose. Now, just one more treat for you, dear." She bent down, placing the comfit at arm's length, and the little thing drew nearer this time. "There you are." Alice shook her finger at it. "No more or you'll spoil your dinner."

"Now, that's settled!" Vincent said. "Are you ready?"

"Certainly." Alice stood to her feet and followed him, brushing sugar from her hands. "That was much better than a game of croquet!"

CHAPTER TEN

I always think that the best way to know God is to love many things.

—Vincent van Gogh

Alice found their direction and off they trudged in much better spirits. She chattered away happily for at least an hour.

But the forest had begun to grow dark and dense, and the darker it grew, the more their conversation dwindled. Trees crowded in on them, casting ghoulish shadows across their path. These were not the tall trees swathed in gentle shoots of flowery vines, nor the sparse ones dotted with seed pods, but heavy trunks with leaves tangled densely and branches tied into gnarled knots.

Alice startled him with a squeal and ran back a few steps. Vincent rounded in alarm, relieved to find it was just that odd, ferret-like creature trundling up behind them.

He walked back to stand beside Alice. "That's what happens when you feed them."

"Then I shall feed them all." She grinned, waiting as it drew nearer.

When it hesitated, she took a cautious step closer and laid another candy down on the ground. "Here you are, little friend."

It grabbed the comfit and scuttled away, nibbling neatly this time instead of gobbling like before. She rejoined Vincent, and they resumed their walk, though she continued to look back over her shoulder.

"Look, it's still following," she said after some time. "We must give it a name. Does it already have one, you think?"

"I imagine this world will name its own things in time. There's no need for us to go around doing it."

"I'm talking about its *name,* not what it's called. For example, I'm called a girl, but my name is Alice. Besides, I already know what it's called. It's a 'tove.'"

"How could you possibly know that?"

"Because of the way it roves about on its toes in that fashion. So, you put the words 'roves' with the word 'toes,' and you get 'toves,' but clearly that's plural, so this is a tove, singular."

She said this with such finality that Vincent didn't even consider contradicting her.

"It is practical, I suppose." He grinned.

"I'm a practical girl." She turned to the tove. "But what to name you?"

"It's not as though we're going to keep it," Vincent said.

"That doesn't mean it doesn't need a name," Alice said. "It would be very rude if we only named the things we kept about us all the time."

Vincent sighed, growing impatient. "OK. What about 'Duke'? It's a good name for a pet." He really just threw it out there hoping they could move on.

"Royalty, then? That might do. I'm sure common toves wouldn't enjoy comfits." She giggled. "Duke it is."

She spun and walked backwards, keeping up with Vincent but watching the little creature as it followed.

"You're going to fall if you go on like that, especially in this tangle of trees we're in." He stopped walking and turned to watch with her. The little tove still trailed behind them with long leaps.

"What do you say, Duke? Are you coming with us all the way?" Alice asked.

It took another leap nearer then stared at her intently, the soft fur twitching about its tiny nose. It stood, its long body wobbling clumsily on its hind legs. "If you'll have me, miss," it said.

Alice gasped and jumped back, never taking her eyes from it. "Vincent! It talks!"

Vincent laughed. "I noticed!"

It continued standing awkwardly, its black eyes somehow both wary and entreating all at once.

Vincent bent down in front of it. "Now, why didn't you say anything earlier?"

"Strangers, sir. It's dangerous in the wood just now. Never know if it's safe." Its tiny voice quavered a little.

"And you don't think the two of us are a danger anymore?" Vincent asked.

"Well,"—it wrung its hands together and passed a gaze back and forth between them—"the miss was very kind and didn't seem to wish me ill. Give me sweets, she did." Its round eyes appealed to her expectantly. "And then you went on your way. Could've, I suppose,"—it laughed nervously—"killed me when you had the chance if you were going to."

"Quite right," Vincent said. "You should be more careful."

"But I was, sir," it said in a wounded tone. "I was playin' dead when she caught me up."

Vincent laughed a huge belly laugh, and the little creature scampered a few steps away from him. "Is that what you were doing?"

"Yes, sir. Supposed to be disguised as a stick, you know, when I'm all stretched out and lyin' still like that." He demonstrated, stretching out straight and rigid on the forest floor.

Alice joined in the laughter but placed a hand over her mouth.

"I see." Vincent cleared his throat and attempted to compose himself. "In that case, you did an excellent job because a stick is just what Alice wanted."

The tove smiled and nodded enthusiastically. "Yes, sir. Thank you, sir."

"Why do you want to come with us?" Alice asked. "Haven't you a family?"

It looked at its feet. "No, miss, not to speak of. And with two giants such as you about, I'd be much safer. You know, what with the danger."

Vincent frowned and stood up. "You shouldn't follow us if that's your reason. We're heading straight for the danger—seeking it out, in fact. If we find it, it'll find you."

The tove's eyes grew wide. "Why would anyone go a-hunting for it?"

"To kill it." Vincent said.

The animal smiled. "Then I've nothing to fear! You'll protect me, just like I said."

"But we mightn't be able to, you know," Alice said, taking her turn to stoop to its level. "No matter what we wish."

"I don't believe it." It shook its head. "I'm sure you're very wise and strong and good. Do let me come."

Alice and the tove both stared at Vincent.

He shrugged. "I suppose we can't keep it from coming if it wants to."

Its shoulders relaxed, and it nodded repeatedly. "Thank you, sir. You won't regret it. I'll do my part."

"I'm sure you will. Now, are you ready to go on?"

"Yes, sir, quite."

"Good."

Vincent resumed their course, Alice lingering behind. A moment later, she reappeared at his side, the tove lounging across her shoulders like a fur stole.

"Oh, Alice…"

"What?" She looked at him wide-eyed as if she had no idea what he referred to.

"It's not a pet."

"But look how short its legs are," she protested. "We can't possibly expect it to go at our speed!"

Vincent shook his head and addressed the creature. "You look remarkably pleased with yourself!"

Its chin lay comfortably in its hands. "She offered, sir. And I have to say, it's most accommodating."

"Carry on, then."

"Now," Alice said, "we named you 'Duke' entirely without your permission. Do you like it? Or did you already have a proper name?"

"'Duke' suits as well as anything. We don't go by names the same as you."

"No?" Alice asked. "How do you call one another?"

"Just the way we sounds to each other. When I cry this way…."—it let out a screeching noise at which Alice put her hand over her ear—"this one knows I want 'em, and when I cry this way…."

"I understand," Alice said. "You needn't demonstrate anymore."

She glanced sidelong at Vincent.

He tried to hold in his laughter. "Regretting your soft heart?"

"Not in the slightest." She straightened as if determined to retain her dignity.

The creature's appearance had taken their mind off the darkening shadows, but the further they delved into the wood, the darker it got. Every now and then, a whisper soughed in the branches above their heads. The bird cries that had sounded so cheerful in the open took on an ominous tone.

"Vincent," Alice said shakily after some minutes in a very dark section, "do you suppose we're quite safe? From everything but the Jabberwock, I mean?"

"I don't think we can be sure of that. It is a forest, after all. There are bound to be creatures we'd rather not meet."

"Yes, I was afraid of that."

Just then, the crunch of leaves sounded from the shadows. Vincent and Alice froze. Duke hopped off Alice's shoulders and cowered beneath a twisted log.

"Just a bird or something, I'm sure," Vincent said, trying to keep his voice steady.

Another rustle, closer now.

Vincent reached for the sword. "Who's there?"

CHAPTER ELEVEN

If I cease searching, then, woe is me, I am lost. That is how I look at it—keep going, keep going come what may.

—Vincent van Gogh

A branch above Vincent's head shook, and he looked up to see a wide-eyed creature with a long, striped tail dangling down behind. He noted that the tove had resumed his stick impersonation, lying motionless on the forest floor.

"Why, it's a sort of cat!" Alice cried.

"A cat, you say?" a voice called down.

"Oh, and it talks!" Alice clapped her hands.

It swished its tail saucily. "A cat…yes. That will do, I think," and a huge grin spread across its wide, furry face.

"My, but I never saw one grin before," Alice said. "They say the Cheshire cats grin from all the milk they get, but I always imagined that was only figurative."

"A Cheshire cat, then?" It grinned even wider, though Vincent would have said that was impossible.

"If it suits you," Alice said. "This is so exciting! A talking cat! It's exactly what I would have wished!" She whispered to Vincent, "Though my Dinah is nicer looking."

"And who's Dinah?" it asked.

"Dinah?" Alice chuckled nervously, obviously wishing the cat hadn't heard. "She's my cat at home. But you are a bit too long and your nose too pointy to make a perfectly good cat. And your eyes are awfully large."

"And where is home?"

"Very far from here," Alice said. "I can't exactly say."

"Well,"—it flicked its tail—"you can't expect animals to look exactly the same everywhere you go."

"No, of course not," Alice said. "I meant no offense."

The cat kept talking. "Anyway, I'm sure your Dinah is too short and too thick. And my eyes are quite the right size." As it said this, they seemed to grow even larger.

"Yes, it's…it's just not what I'm used to." The words spilled out of Alice's mouth in a rush. "I hope you'll forgive me."

"Hmm," it said, "it doesn't matter anyway."

Alice tried again. "Do you have a name, Cheshire cat? We can't go on just calling you that."

"Why not?"

"There may be a hundred different Cheshire cats!" Alice said.

"There is no one like me, I assure you."

"Well, if you're happy with it, I suppose it will do," she said, shrugging.

It stared disinterestedly out into the forest as if she hadn't spoken at all, then changed the subject entirely. "So, what brings you into the Tulgey Wood?"

"Is that what this place is called?" Alice scanned their surroundings. "It's a bit gloomy. The name suits it, though."

Vincent was glad she hadn't answered the cat directly. It made him uncomfortable, though he couldn't have said why. He asked his own question. "What can you tell us about this Tulgey Wood? Anything we ought to know? Monsters ahead or the like?" Vincent attempted to sound casual. "We saw something dead a little way back. Thought maybe you'd know if we ought to be worried."

The cat seemed indifferent. "Well, you're bound to run across dead things in a forest. Everything must die."

"Yes, but something killed this creature," Vincent said.

"Oh, that is another matter. Killing is a gruesome business." The cat shuddered dramatically. "Though, it isn't quite fair to those who must kill to eat, is it?"

Vincent frowned.

"That is true," Alice said. "Nurse makes me put a bell 'round Dinah's neck so she can't sneak up on the little birds. Calls her a brute and all sorts of ugly names when she catches things though Dinah can't help it one bit."

"Exactly," the Cheshire cat said, grinning broadly.

"I don't think it's quite the same," Vincent said. He was liking the cat less and less.

"But have you seen anything dangerous in the forest?" Alice asked, then whispered to Vincent, "Cats see a great many things, you know."

"Many dangerous things, yes," it said.

"In which direction?" Alice continued.

"That way." Its arms reached across one another and pointed in opposite directions.

"Well, that's not very specific," Alice said.

"It's a forest, dear. There's danger every way. I could be much more exact if you were to tell me, say, which direction you planned to go, and if I knew your purpose—well, perhaps I could even show you the way."

Vincent shook his head at Alice vehemently.

She hesitated then asked, "Well, can you at least tell us which way we ought to go from here?"

"That depends a good deal on where you want to get to," said the cat.

"I'm afraid we don't exactly know where we're going."

"Then it doesn't matter which way you go," it said.

"Well, we'd like to get somewhere."

"You're sure to do that if you only walk long enough."

"Now, Cheshire Cat," Alice said, a hint of frustration in her voice, "maybe we could try it a different way. Can you tell us what we might find if we go that way?" She pointed to her right.

"Stinging things with giant wings."

Alice shuddered. "That doesn't sound nice at all." She pointed to her left. "And that way?"

"Scaly beasts with chomping teeth."

"Oh, dear…."

"I wouldn't go the way you're headed, either," the Cheshire cat said. "Everyone who goes that way ends up mad."

"But I don't want to go among mad people," Alice said.

"Oh, you can't help that," the cat said, its grin growing to alarming proportions. "We're all mad here. I'm mad. You're mad." He pointed at Vincent with his tail. "He's definitely mad."

"We'll take our chances." Vincent nodded curtly. "Thank you for your kind assistance."

"Don't say I didn't warn you," the cat said.

Alice curtsied to the cat as it veered off, heading deeper into the forest. They had gone several paces when she looked back over her shoulder. "Vincent! I was going to ask that cat a question, but it's not there! Where could it have gone so quickly?"

Vincent turned to see nothing at all. "I don't care. Good riddance."

She frowned. "What's wrong with you?"

"I don't like that cat or whatever it is. I think it's one of those creatures I'd rather not meet in the forest."

"But it could talk!" Alice protested.

"Yes, and I didn't like it any better for all that." He looked down at Duke who stood next to Alice's leg now.

"Duke didn't like it either, for the record. Played dead the whole time."

"Oh, Duke played dead when we came around as well. The cat's just a mischievous old thing, surely. And the rabbit said only the animals we needed on our way would be able to talk, so surely, it's meant to help. Cats get a bad reputation—even our own cats, and they aren't half so wild as that one."

"The rabbit also said the Jabberwock could take any form, remember? I don't think we should trust every creature that crosses our pathway."

"Well,"—Alice frowned—"I have to admit I wasn't excessively fond of its grin."

"Indeed!" Vincent said. "I thought the ends of its mouth would meet in the back, and its head might come off altogether!"

"Oh, that would be awful!" Alice said.

They resumed their walk in an uncomfortable silence. Vincent couldn't stop thinking of all the dangers the cat had mentioned and felt certain Alice was doing the same. He could practically see her spirits falling in the gloom.

"I wish we could go back," she said, her voice sounding inordinately loud in the eerie stillness of the Tulgey Wood. "At least into the cheerful part of the forest. And I am getting hungry."

"I wouldn't turn down a meal, either, but there's probably not an inn up ahead, so we may as well keep walking."

The trees finally thinned, and the light grew brighter, but their long, tedious walk had taken its toll. Feet were weary, energy flagged, and Vincent wondered if Alice felt as lost as he did. He didn't have to wonder for long.

"Oh, Vincent," she finally said. "Maybe I can't find anything! Surely, we should have arrived somewhere by now!" She covered her face with her hands.

He agreed but didn't say so. "We'll come to something eventually, Alice." He looked around for any hint of a direction. And then he saw it. "Oh, no."

"What?" Alice raised her head sharply.

Vincent pointed without a word.

The rabbit's hollow tree stood in front of them. They were right back where they started.

CHAPTER TWELVE

The beginning is perhaps more difficult than anything else, but keep heart; it will turn out all right.

—Vincent van Gogh

"It can't be!" Alice jumped up and ran toward the hollow tree. She parted the branches covering its opening and disappeared inside.

Vincent followed closely behind. "It can't be, but it is."

Alice sat down on the floor and began to cry despite the fact that a lovely tray of bread and butter with a steaming pot of tea sat in the corner.

Vincent knelt beside her. He remembered the sword this time and swept the tip to the side as he bent so it wouldn't knock him over like before. "Don't cry, Alice. We'll figure it out."

He placed his hand on hers, and the touch woke his vision. Everything in sight wavered, colors running together like wet paint on a palette. The normally fiery eddies around Alice dulled and sank slowly to her feet as if weighed down.

Not as bad as after we saw the dead animal, but still....

"Something to eat and drink will help." He stood and walked over to the table. A note lay on the edge of the tray. He prepared a cup of tea for Alice and handed it to her absentmindedly, his eyes on the note in his other hand.

"What's that?" she asked.

"A note."

"Well, what's it say?"

He read it aloud. "Humans are so likely to go in circles, I've left you a meal. Remember, you will only get where you want to go. Focus."

He looked into Alice's miserable eyes.

"It's my fault!" She set her tea on the floor and covered her face, hiding new tears. "That pitiful, lifeless beast upset me so, and I didn't want to find the Jabberwock anymore, and then I said I wanted to go back and that I wanted dinner, and now we've done both, but we've lost our way!"

Vincent noticed Duke trembling near the doorway.

"Don't cry about it, Alice," he said again. "Now, we know. We'll just have to be purposeful from here on, that's all. Like the rabbit said." He glanced up at the tove. "And I think you're scaring Duke."

Alice nodded and sniffled. "Yes. I'll just focus very particularly on where we need to go in the end instead of wishing for what I'd like at the moment." She wiped the tears from her face and looked at the tove. "I'm sorry, Duke. It will work out. I just know it will." She took the candy tin from her pocket. "Would you like another sweet?" She passed the tove several more candies at its enthusiastic nod, then stood and dusted herself off. "Now, is that bread and butter over there?"

She and Vincent ate and drank everything on the tray, and the meal went a long way towards restoring their spirits.

Alice peeked her head back out into the forest. "It's already getting dark, Vincent. Do you suppose we shall have to give it up without making any progress at all today?"

"I think we might as well stay here and continue in the morning."

"But a whole day wasted!" Her shoulders slumped. "Now that I've eaten, I think I could walk all night if we needed to. I'm quite fixed on…on finding. And mightn't we go on at night? You can guide us in the dark with your sight, can't you?"

"Maybe," he said, doubtfully. "But we have to sleep sometime, after all. It might as well be here instead of out in the open."

She reluctantly agreed.

"But I think we should try something," Vincent added.

"OK."

"You said maybe you got off track because you didn't really want to find the Jabberwock anymore, right?"

"Yes."

"So, what if you tried to find something else?

"But what would I look for instead?" she asked.

"What if you tried to find more of the animals we're to meet along the way? You're still excited about that, I'll warrant."

She grinned. "Oh, yes. That's just what I am looking forward to." She cocked her head and looked up at the tops of the trees. "Do you think I could, though? I wouldn't know what to look for. I've only searched for objects when I knew what I wanted to find. How can I find something if I don't know what it is?"

"That's what we're going to test," he said. "I'll go hide something, and I won't tell you what it is."

"That's brilliant, Vincent!"

She followed him back out of the hollow tree, Duke at their heels.

"Now," he said, "cover your eyes so you can't see."

"OK." She rounded and hid her face against a tree. "Make it difficult or it won't count."

"All right," Vincent said. "Now, count to one hundred."

She nodded.

"Aloud," he added.

"I'm not going to cheat, Vincent! This is a serious experiment, not hide-and-go-seek."

He grinned.

So she thinks.

He quietly pulled a vial of tea from his pocket and drank it down slowly.

Don't want to overdo it! What might happen if you drank too much? Would you shrink away altogether?

Duke opened his mouth in shock as Vincent began to shrink but seemed to understand the secret and said nothing.

By the time Vincent's height stabilized, he was so small that a blade of grass arced over his head. He stepped stealthily through the underbrush. Something like a ladybug hung from the bottom of a leaf. The sheen on its shell gleamed like a glass figurine, reflecting his face back to him. He couldn't resist reaching out a hand to touch it and marveled at its smoothness.

Alice spoke louder as she neared the end of her countdown. "Ninety-five, ninety-six...."

He had just scrambled under the awning of a larger-leafed plant when an alarming thought struck him.

Suppose she tramples me underfoot?

He rushed to a nearby bush and climbed it frantically just as she called out, "One-hundred!"

Vincent strained to pull himself to each branch until he reached a height of about two feet from the ground. He peeked at Alice from behind the leaves.

What fun shrinking would be in our own world!

"Vincent!" she called. "Did you hide something?" Concern passed over her face. "Vincent?"

He laughed silently, though he didn't think Alice could hear him anyway at his size.

"It's not funny, Vincent!" She stamped. "Where did he go, Duke?"

"I can't say, miss!" Duke responded, though Vincent thought he looked a bit shamefaced as he said it.

Clever thing. Not even really a lie!

"Oh!" Alice said. "I suppose he's gone and hidden himself just as if it *were* a game of hide-and-go-seek. No matter." She straightened her dress. "I'll find him."

She closed her eyes and put her gloved hands out, touching the nearest tree. Her face twisted up in concentration. She smiled and pulled her hand away. She took three short steps to the bush, reached down and parted the branches, her great eyes peering at him from above.

"Oh, Vincent! Look how tiny you are!" She squealed.

And to his horror, she reached down and picked him up, placing him in the palm of her hand. The rapid ascent took his breath away.

"Alice!" He gasped. "Put me down!" He didn't dare peer over the edge of her hand at that great height.

"But you are cute, Vincent!" She giggled. "You're no bigger than a chessman, and your voice sounds just like a little mouse! I wish I could always have a Vincent to put in my pocket and carry around with me."

"Alice!" he yelled.

"Oh, all right." She lowered her hand to the ground and let him climb off. "I suppose it wouldn't be proper." She grinned at him, stooping so they could talk. "At least we know it works," she said.

"No, we don't," he said. "You worked out I was hiding myself and knew exactly what to look for. Experiment failed."

Her face clouded. "Of course, you're right." She stood and covered her eyes. "Go again, then."

She began to count.

This time Vincent picked up a purple berry he found on the ground. He could hardly lift it at his size but managed to lug it over to the trailing roots of the nearest tree and shove it in a small hollow.

The sweet smell of the berry dazzled his senses—more tempting than any apple tart his mother had ever baked in the hearth.

Might be poisonous. I'll ask Duke when we're done.

He climbed to the top of the root, running up it to get as near the tree trunk as possible.

She still may flatten me if I'm out in the open.

Alice's count ended, and the entire scenario repeated. She took longer this time, her face filled with consternation until it finally broke into a sunny grin.

Vincent watched from his perch on the root, leaning against the trunk of the tree.

"I've got it!" She opened her eyes and ran to the root, knelt down, and pulled out the berry, a little purple juice dripping down her hand as she worked it out of the little hole. Her fingers were much larger than Vincent's. "And I know where you are, too, Vincent!" She shifted her gaze to him.

He smiled. "OK, *now* we know it works, and I'm going back to my right size."

He took a bite of cake, then a bit more until he grew to a reasonable height. "That's better." He brushed the crumbs from his hands.

"You ought not waste the tea and cakes like that, Vincent," Alice scolded. "We haven't any idea how often we'll need them."

But she said it so optimistically that her words barely stung.

She turned to the tove. "This berry smells divine, Duke. Can we eat it?"

"Just what I was going to ask," Vincent said.

"Oh, I wouldn't. You'd be doubled over with stomach pains, miss."

"Hmm." Alice sighed and dropped the berry. "Pity. The most tempting things are always the worst, aren't they?" She wiped two purple fingertips on her skirt. "Now, before we go on, we have one more experiment. I haven't tried seeking while wearing the gloves and holding your hand at the same time, Vincent. Was it very different for you? The difference between only the blindfold and when I touched your hand as well?"

"Very." He nodded.

"Then I'd better see for myself!" She put one hand back on the tree and stretched out the other to him.

He took it, ignoring the onslaught to his own senses, and watched as she closed her eyes and crinkled her nose.

A wide smile broadened across her face, and she released his hand, opening her eyes wide. "Incredible!"

"Different then?" Vincent asked.

"It's the difference between an ancient pathway grown over with shrubbery and a brand new one paved with bricks! I couldn't mistake it if I tried!"

The night was nearly upon them now, and they re-entered the hollow tree.

Alice glanced warily around the shadowy interior—an action Vincent could only see in silhouette. He felt certain he knew what Alice was feeling. "It's not going to be nearly as cozy as last night, I'm afraid."

"No," Alice said. "No light, no beds." She took his hand, and the world lit up for him. "Can you see it now?" she asked.

"Yes."

"Good," she said. "At least one of us will be able to see—until we fall asleep, anyway."

He could see her smile in a whirl of color.

So, they sat, backs to the rough wall, holding hands, Duke curled up between them. Once again, Vincent lay awake long after he heard Alice's steady breathing. He could almost get used to this sight as it was now. Here, in the dark with no one watching his reactions, he could allow himself to drink it in.

CHAPTER THIRTEEN

In fighting the difficulties, the inmost strength of the heart is developed.

—Vincent van Gogh

Sore backs and stiff necks woke them early, but the morning was not without delight.

"Vincent, look!" Alice cried nearly the minute she opened her eyes.

A fresh tea tray awaited them, complete with warm biscuits and jam, wisps of steam rising from the teapot.

"How could the rabbit possibly know?" Alice asked, eyes twinkling.

Vincent shrugged. "Like you said, he might not be a wizard, but he's something."

And they fell to with no hesitation.

"We mustn't waste any more time," Alice said as she tilted her teacup high to get the last drop.

"I'm quite ready," Vincent said.

They stepped out into the open, and Alice walked to the same tree she'd touched the morning before. "I won't get off track this time, Vincent. I'll be perfectly steadfast." She put her hand on the tree and closed her eyes. "Give me your hand so I haven't any doubt of the way."

He did as she asked, and she smiled broadly then opened her eyes. "Follow me!"

Duke trundled along beside as they retraced their steps, the noisy cacophony of birdsong making the world feel lively and cheerful. Alice led them the long way around to avoid seeing the body of the little creature again, and Vincent was glad of it.

She seemed more intent and serious than she had the day before.

Worried about getting lost again.

He did not attempt conversation. He was just as happy with the silence.

Alice finally plopped down on a mossy patch beneath a dark tree and sighed. She pointed ahead where the shadows grew darker and the branches seemed like gangly arms grasping every which way. "I'm not fond of the Tulgey Wood."

"No," he said. "Neither am I. But if that's where we go, it's where we go." He looked at her intently. "Are you OK?"

"I suppose. Just afraid I'll get mixed up again. In there is where I got turned around before, and I'm not any more excited about the options the cat gave us than I was then."

Vincent frowned. "So, it was the cat that scared you off track?"

"Well, it's not the cat's fault if it's just telling us what's out there, but I am certain that's where I went wrong. And you can't be excited about stinging things or scaly beasts or madness, either!

"No, but those can't be worse than the Jabberwock itself, and that's what we're headed for."

"I know, I know." She stood up. "Forget it. Let's just go."

She stalked into the Tulgey Wood before he had gotten all the way to his feet.

Vincent trotted to catch up, but Alice walked quickly in that tangled wood, and before Vincent reached her, he heard a scuffle in the trees nearby. He stopped and saw Alice do the same. She looked at him, eyes wide.

Then he saw it.

The Cheshire Cat sauntered up in a tree nearby.

Vincent's jaw tightened. "Oh, it's you."

"Don't be rude, Vincent!" Alice said.

The cat's eyes scanned the area. Vincent realized that Duke was playing dead again and decided to start walking.

If Duke doesn't want to be noticed, I'm not going to let that cat see him.

"Vincent!" Alice called. "Where are you going?"

"We need to keep moving, Alice. I think our friend can keep up." He pointed at the cat, but shifted his eyes back toward Duke, hoping she'd get the point.

"If you say so." She frowned. "A bit rude, though."

The cat followed along, hopping from limb to limb as they walked. "How are you getting on?" it asked.

"Well…" Alice said, "that's hard to say. We got lost after meeting you yesterday and simply made a huge circle. So, today, we've started over, which is really the best thing you can do when you've gone off track."

"Is it?" the cat purred. "But how do you know you won't go in a circle again?"

"I'm being much more attentive today," Alice said.

Vincent let her do the talking. He didn't like the cat's tone and didn't see a reason to interact with it.

"Hmm," the cat said. "It seems you're going in exactly the direction you did yesterday, so who's to say you haven't already gone off track again?"

"Oh," Alice said, "well, of course, it's possible, but one can't go thinking that way all the time or you'd never get anywhere."

"Too true." The cat hopped lithely to the next tree. "Well, I suppose you'll have a difficult decision when you reach our meeting point from yesterday. After all, from there, it's danger every way except back the way you came."

Vincent glanced at Alice's face and was relieved to see her mouth form a determined line.

"I suppose it is," Alice said, "but we'll go on regardless once we figure out the way. Some things are more important than keeping oneself safe."

The cat jumped to a tree a little further off. "Such bravery…." Its voice trailed off as it sauntered away. "I hope it is rewarded."

Alice whirled on Vincent as soon as the cat was out of sight, but he held a finger over his mouth. "Not yet, Alice. Just keep walking," he hissed.

He heard her exhale sharply and turned to see her looking back over her shoulder.

When he felt sure the cat was gone, he spoke. "I'm sorry, Alice. I told you I don't like that cat. The more it talks, the less I like it, and I didn't want it to see Duke. What if he's its prey or something?"

"Well, how's Duke going to find us now?" Alice stopped. "We've got to go back and find him."

"No, we don't. He's an animal after all; I'm sure he can track things just like other animals do, and he might've been following all along. Give him a minute."

She huffed.

"Why don't you make sure we're still on the right track in the meantime?" Vincent asked. Mostly, he just wanted to give her something to distract her from being mad at him.

"Fine." She put her hand on a tree and concentrated.

Vincent took the opportunity while she was silent. "I was proud of what you said to the cat."

Alice opened her eyes. "What did I say?"

"That some things are more important than keeping yourself safe. You didn't let the stinging things and everything it mentioned yesterday get to you."

She smiled. "Well, I hope I haven't. I guess we'll find out if I take us in a humongous circle again."

"Miss?" a voice called as a wriggling black nose poked itself through the brush at their feet.

"Oh, Duke!" Alice reached down and stroked his nose. "I was worried we'd lost you forever."

"Not at all, miss. I'd be able to smell you miles away."

She straightened when it said this. "Smell me? Really!" She stomped away.

Vincent laughed and caught up to her.

"That was very rude," she said.

"I'm sure it meant no disrespect. Think of your finding gift and my seeing, and imagine if your sense of smell was as strong as either of them."

"I really meant no harm, miss." Duke stood a few feet away. "It's not to say you smell unpleasant-like. It's a nice fishy odor."

"Oh!" Alice's face flushed, and she ran ahead, leaving both of them behind.

"Did I say something wrong, sir?" Duke asked Vincent. "I find fishes very agreeable."

Vincent laughed until his eyes watered. "There's no accounting what a lady will take offense to, Duke."

Alice slowed and turned around only minutes later. "Come here, Duke. I'm sorry I was cross, and I'm happy you're back."

She even gave him another candy and let him hop up on her shoulder again.

They ducked under low branches, sidestepped clumps of tangled vines, and Vincent had jumped at more than one shadow by the time he recognized their surroundings. One large, sprawling tree splayed out in front of them, a set of three hollows in its trunk giving the impression of a particularly ghoulish, gawping face. This was where they'd met the cat yesterday. He stopped and looked at Alice. "Want to test our direction?"

She took a deep breath. "Yes, I suppose we must. Give me your hand again."

"OK," Vincent said, "but first, let's do something. Come here."

She walked over to him.

"Now, close your eyes," —he took her by the shoulders and spun her around and around—"and keep them closed."

"Vincent!" she protested.

"If you don't know which way you're facing, you can't be influenced by what the cat said yesterday."

He took one of her hands and placed it on the nearest tree, taking the other in his own.

She swayed on her feet. "Yes, I'm sure that's sensible, but I am dizzy."

Alice, eyes still closed, took her arm off the tree and pointed. "I think it's that way." She opened one eye. "Oh, dear." Her shoulders slumped. "I was hoping it wasn't madness."

CHAPTER FOURTEEN

Be clearly aware of the stars and infinity on high.
Then life seems almost enchanted after all.

—Vincent van Gogh

They hadn't walked many steps before Alice put a hand on Vincent's arm. "We're also going to need to be much smaller."

"Smaller?" Vincent peered at her doubtfully. "How do you know?"

"Didn't I say? I get a sort of a sense as to what's to come."

"No, you didn't say! You mean you can tell the future?"

She shook her head decidedly. "Nothing so specific as that! Just a little nudge."

"All right." He took one of the vials of shrinking tea from his pocket. "How small, then?"

Alice pursed her lips. "Bottoms up, I think."

They drank their vials together.

Vincent watched the world around him grow larger and larger until the tove itself became the size of a veritable monster.

"My!" Duke said. "I suppose I shall have to protect you two now!"

"It's only temporary," Alice said.

"I shan't mind. Turnabout's fair play."

Alice peered at Vincent around a weed. "This is a very odd feeling. I should think we're no more than three inches high!"

"Yes," Vincent said. "Imagine if a giant five feet high picked you up!"

She giggled. "You deserved it for tricking me."

"Well, we'd best get moving. We won't make any time at all at this height. Lead the way, Alice." He fell into step beside her. "Any idea how far it is?"

"It must not be terribly far," she said, "or we'd have been better off at our proper size. This is definitely not the most efficient means of travel. Every root seems like a giant tree felled across our path!"

"Yes," Vincent agreed. "Do you think this is what it's like to go exploring in the untamed Amazon jungles?"

"It's very like I would imagine!" Alice pushed a stalk of tall grass out of her path.

But the journey was longer than expected, and they struggled through the jungle of leaves and weeds and fallen twigs.

Conversation had long-since ceased when Alice cried out and jumped back.

"What is it?" Vincent ran forward.

"I think it's harmless, but it is startling." Alice pointed. "It's the size of a cat, after all!"

A beetle lumbered by, glancing at them stupidly.

"It's beautiful." Vincent lost himself in the vision. "Like seeing one of the water bugs on my pond up close." The lights danced off its shell, casting green and blue glimmers all around.

Alice took his hand with no warning, magnifying the otherworldly sensation.

Vincent gasped in amazement. The beetle shone like ribbons of prismatic color caught in a rushing stream. This vision showed him more than just pretty colors; he could see what the beetle felt. It radiated a magnificent joy Vincent never would have suspected, reveling in its simple existence.

Alice released his hand, and he found that a tear trickled down his cheek.

He brushed it away. "Thank you. I...I don't think I'd have asked to see it that way, but I'm glad I did. The beetles always fascinated me."

She smiled at him. "And look,"—she pointed through the thick tangle of weeds—"I think it clears up ahead!"

"Yes! I think you're right!" Open sky peeked between a far line of trees. "Maybe that's our destination."

They only progressed a little further before they came upon a train of something like very large ants blocking their path. They marched in single file, the line stretching as far as the eye could see in either direction.

"I hardly dare step over them like I normally would," Alice said.

"Definitely not," Vincent agreed, eyeing their mandibles. "I don't fancy one of those pincers latching on to my ankle!"

"I could hop you over if you like," Duke said. "Just climb on my back, and we'll be off!"

"That's a fabulous idea, Duke!" Alice said. "But I think twilight is coming on, don't you, Vincent? And if so, there's no need to rush." She just kept talking without giving Vincent a chance to answer. "We've been walking for ever so long. Let's just get to the edge of the clearing then call it a day. Is that all right?"

"Yes, certainly," Vincent answered.

They sat on the branch of a low bush to watch the procession go by. Several minutes passed, and they still couldn't see the end.

"My, but they're taking their time," Alice said. "You'd think they could learn to go all at once instead of behaving like the forest had a queue!"

Vincent laughed. "Agreed." But he grew somber again as his mind turned to their gifts.

"Alice, how does it feel when you use your gift?"

"Well," she pondered for a moment, "it's sort of as if an invisible string pulls me along just like a little tug boat. When I'm uncertain of it, it seems like a hundred strings are pulling me in different directions. I just try to hold on to the strongest one. I think that's why I lost my way yesterday. I really did want to go back, so the string leading me back felt the most solid. Since then, I've been very careful not to let my fears keep me from following the right way."

"And what about when you're not using it?" Vincent asked.

"That's hard to say as I'm really trying to use it all the time since I got us lost. If I don't stay focused like the rabbit said, I might go wrong again."

"Is it bothersome?" Vincent said. "Trying to use it constantly like that?"

"Only when I'm very conflicted. Then, it's like the threads could quite pull me apart—like all the ways I might go are fighting over me, and to follow the one, I have to fight against all the others. That's the draining part. But when I'm attending to the right way and don't heed the ones trying to drag me off track, it becomes more natural. And I'm sure the longer I do that, the easier it will become. Does that make sense?" She didn't pause to let him answer. "And it must make me awfully hungry. I could already do with another snack!"

Duke piped up. "These bugs are actually quite tasty, miss. Want me to grab a few?"

Alice grimaced. "That's...um...another delightful suggestion, Duke, but it's not the sort of thing humans eat."

"No?" Duke's eyes widened. "Well, to each his own."

Vincent would've liked to continue the conversation about their gifts, but Alice hopped up just then and dusted off her dress.

"Oh, good! There's the end. I was just about to say we might climb on Duke's back and hop over after all, but here it is."

It took them no time at all to reach the edge of the tree line once they were on the move, and as the landscape opened before them, Vincent drank in the splendor.

A field spread across the horizon, awash with blue flowers waving in the wind like a rolling sea. The ground sloped down into the field, and their vantage point allowed full view of the breathtaking expanse.

"This is magnificent!" Alice exclaimed.

Vincent stood speechless.

"It's going to be perfectly exquisite strolling into a forest of flowers, Vincent!" Alice practically squealed in delight. "Just like walking on the bottom of the sea! A wonderland, indeed!"

She grabbed his arm, and at her touch the image sprang into life causing the field to roil as if it really were an ocean.

It wasn't the first time the beauty of his sight had astonished him, but this surpassed anything he could imagine. The sapphire sky intermingled with the sea of indigo flowers, hypnotizing him with its vitality. Golden-white stars dappled Sian's strange dusk, sending whorls of light spiraling out in a thousand shades of twilight.

"It looks like I could swim right through it!" he cried.

Alice took her hand away. "Pretty, isn't it?" She smiled mischievously and gave him a teasing glance.

"You did that on purpose," he said. "And with the beetle earlier, too."

"Well…yes. You seem a bit uncertain about your gift."

"I never said…."

"You didn't have to." She didn't let him finish. "I see those dark moods passing when you think I'm not paying attention. Your feelings practically hang above your head on a placard."

"Oh…." He felt his face reddening and looked at his feet.

"Don't be ashamed of it. I shouldn't like it if you changed. Most people keep everything so stuffed away."

He smiled. "I think so, too. I can't imagine how they live that way. I know I couldn't. My feelings just boil over like a pot. But don't you think me strange? Everyone else does."

She frowned. "'Everyone' doesn't know everything, all squished up in their own heads like they are. They don't know about this place, do they?"

Vincent smiled. "No, unless they're very good at keeping fantastic secrets."

"And they'd think us mad if we told them," Alice said, "but they'd be wrong."

Vincent smiled.

"So, if they tell you you're strange," Alice continued, "you just remember they don't know everything, and they're often wrong. I think you're extraordinary. And to be extraordinary is, by definition, to be something other than ordinary. And if one isn't ordinary, I'm afraid one might very often feel out of place. So, promise me, Vincent. Promise me you won't let them make you ordinary."

"I'll try, Alice."

"That's good enough." She straightened her dress. "Now, I'm starving. Can you tell us what we might eat, Duke?"

"Certainly, miss. I can even fetch something if you like." He ran off before she could reply.

"Hmm." Alice frowned. "I wanted to tell him not to bring anything that wriggles. If he thought those ant-things would've made a good meal, there's no telling what he may bring back."

Duke returned a few minutes later with some kind of nut. He dropped it in front of them.

"Well, that seems all right, then." Alice smiled.

"Yes, and it's large enough to feed us at our current height," Vincent said. "It's the size of a pumpkin." He rapped the shell with his knuckles. "It's tough as a walnut, though. I don't know if I can crack it."

"Give it over, sir," the tove said.

Vincent handed it up. The tove took it in his little paws and held it to its mouth. His sharp teeth and powerful jaws cracked the tough shell with no trouble at all.

Duke examined the halves and handed one to each of them.

Vincent smiled, noting the larger half went to Alice. He unstrapped the sword, flinching at the sore spots on his shoulders where the scabbard had begun to rub blisters, then sat down to his dinner.

"Did you get none for yourself, Duke?" Alice asked.

"I can eat about twenty of those in a minute, miss. I ate while I was roving about. Quite stuffed." He eyed her expectantly. "Though I wouldn't say no to one of those sweets."

Alice laughed. "I'd gladly share them, but we should, perhaps, wait until we aren't quite so small. Right now, they'd be about the size of a grain of sand to you."

"Quite right, miss," the tove said dejectedly.

Vincent found a bit of the shell that had fallen and used it to pry out apple-sized pieces of the nut, but it still proved quite the chore.

"It's tremendously chewy," Alice said with a mouthful, "and quite dry."

"Yes, it would be far better baked into a pie," Vincent agreed.

After eating his fill, he laid back and put his head in his hands. They were camped on a mossy knoll just inside the tree line, the open sky clearly visible between the massive trunks.

"It is lovely here, Vincent," Alice said.

"Mm-hmm."

Alice laid down as well and rolled her head on the grass to look at him. "I used to read fairy stories, you know, but never imagined the things in them could actually happen. I'll write a story about this one day. I'll call it *Adventures in Wonderland*."

Vincent laughed. "Nobody would believe it."

"Of course not! No one but the children, at any rate. And I'd add a lot more nonsense just for fun."

"You think you would need more?"

"No." She laughed. "But I've so many ideas. I could include all my dreams. I have very vivid ones, you know. In one, the kings and queens from the chess set get into a war with the kings and queens on my deck of cards. And in another, a baby turns into a pig right before my eyes." She faced the sky again. "Vincent?"

"Yes?"

"I want you to tell me what the sky looks like...what it *really* looks like. Will you?"

"Yes,"—he paused for a moment—"but not with the blindfold."

"Deal." She reached over and grabbed his hand.

The intense flood to his senses still sent him reeling, but concentrating on how to explain it to Alice helped rein in the chaos.

"Will it matter that it's mostly dark?" she asked.

"Not a bit. I'm not really using my eyes, like you said. Now, look straight between those two trees." He pointed. "You see that cloud?"

"Yes."

"It's billowing like a flag on a ship's mast. It's not only white or gray, but the blue from the sky and the yellow from the starlight drifts into it the way milk rolls into your tea. And the trees reach into the sky with living fingers, leaves glowing like fireflies. The light infuses everything—the world seems made of it. Everything is brimming with life the way my pond is if you take the time to look, shimmering, colors streaming from one thing into the next. It's like the plants are talking with one another, and the trees are talking with the sky." He looked over at her. "Do you want to know what you look like?"

"If you want to tell me," she said.

"You're made of fire."

"What do you mean?"

"You're all aflame with red and orange, and you glow just like a firelight."

An extra shot of red spun through the swirls of light around her face.

A smile.

"And Duke?" she asked.

"Duke is green and brown, reaching deep into the earth as if he had roots like the trees." Vincent sighed. "I'm not sure I'm very good at describing it. It would be far better as a painting."

"Is it easier now, Vincent? Does it still scare you?"

"Not as much. Normally, it comes over me all at once, like the whole world's a living thing, and it's somehow inside of me. When I describe it in words, I can sort of step outside of it."

"Then do that, Vincent. Step outside of it and look at it from there."

He let go of her hand. "Every time I use it, my vision—my regular vision—is changed more. The edges of things are going all fuzzy. I'm scared it won't go back to normal when we return home."

"For my part," Alice said, "I wouldn't want it to! It would be very useful to always find whatever I needed!" She paused. "Finding things is very ordinary, though. Your gift is brilliant. I hope you come to love it."

"I don't know if I can, Alice. It's so strong sometimes I almost feel I am going to explode from within."

"Don't fear it, Vincent. If you feel that way, it is only because you are seeing so much more of the world than anyone else, and that is no punishment. Think of what you could do with vision like that."

What could I possibly do? Seeing isn't doing. It doesn't affect anything at all.

CHAPTER FIFTEEN

There is nothing more beautiful than nature early in the morning.

—Vincent van Gogh

Vincent woke just as dawn peered over the distant hills, its light falling over the calm sea of flowers like a blanket. Alice still slept, and Duke was somewhere out of sight.

Off to find something to eat, most likely.

Vincent's stomach rumbled.

He tried not to wake Alice, creeping silently over to the remainder of last night's dinner. He munched absentmindedly while watching the sunrise. He considered whether he should practice with the blindfold, but the incredible view in front of him seemed almost too beautiful as it was, and he couldn't shake the fear he may lose this normal vision altogether.

Better enjoy it while I can.

The rosy hue the morning cast over the blue flowers turned them a deep lavender. As the light grew stronger, the blue reasserted itself. The field lay placid and unmoving this morning in contrast to its windswept waves of the evening before.

Sunbeams fell across Alice's face, and she stirred, waking just as Duke returned.

"'Morning, miss," Duke said.

"Good morning, Duke." She yawned and added, "Good morning, Vincent."

He smiled but didn't speak.

She joined him at picking on the bits of nut.

"Awfully quiet, isn't it?" She shaded her eyes with her hand and perused the treetops. "The birds were making a thunderous racket at sunrise the other mornings."

"I know," Vincent said. "Back home, a field like this would be filled with animals of all kinds. Now that the wind died down, the flowers are as still as statues. Any ideas, Duke?"

"No, sir. I've always stayed in the forest. More places to hide."

"Ah, well. No matter." Alice stretched out her arm like a cat. "I'll tell you what is the matter, though. I'm terribly parched. You were awfully handy about the food, Duke, but I wish we had some water."

"There are the dramberries if you're thirsty."

"What are they?" Alice asked.

"Little yellow berries full of juice. It's what we eat if we gets thirsty and there's no water about."

"And there are some nearby?" Vincent asked.

"Yes, sir. I found a patch while roaming this morning. Would you like me to go fetch you some?"

"By all means!" Vincent's mouth felt as dry as burnt toast.

Duke scuttered away and returned a few minutes later with empty hands.

"Were they all gone, Duke?" Alice asked.

Duke mumbled, but they couldn't understand him.

And then Vincent realized why. Duke opened his mouth, and several yellow berries covered in saliva fell out at Alice's feet.

Vincent nearly collapsed with laughter at her look of absolute horror, but she recovered quickly.

"Oh, um, thank you, Duke. I'm sure they're quite… delicious," she stammered.

Vincent couldn't resist. He strode over and picked one up—it took both hands at his current size—and bit into it heartily.

"Vincent!" Alice cried. "That's absolutely…."—she glanced up at the tove's face and hesitated—"…well, how is it anyway?"

And though he'd done it only to shock her, he said, truthfully, "It's the most delicious fruit I've ever eaten and just bursting with juice. You have to eat some no matter the…you know."

"What's it like?"

"Better than the finest strawberry you've ever tasted!"

"Oh…" she said. "I am very thirsty. And you're sure it's alright?"

"You won't regret it." His second mouthful muffled the words.

She put one hand on a berry and attempted to wipe a clean spot before nibbling it dubiously.

"You've got to bite into it, Alice," he said. "Did you even break the skin?"

"Oh, all right." She set her face with determination. Her first real taste clearly won her over, and she ate with no more hesitation. She wiped her mouth as she finished. "I only wish I could have another!"

"I know! If we were at our right size, we could eat a basketful at once!"

"To be sure!" she said. "Now, let's go. I'll check we're still on track if you'll give me your hand."

He did so, wiping it on his pants first, a little embarrassed at the stickiness left from the dramberry.

"Yes," she said, "definitely down into that field of flowers."

Something occurred to Vincent. "Alice, why do you suppose we needed to shrink yesterday? We haven't come across any more speaking animals. For that matter, why didn't we shrink before meeting Duke? I thought that was the point—so the animals wouldn't attack us in defense."

"Hmm, there's bound to be a reason. I bet...with Duke, I needed to give him the comfits so he'd know we meant no harm, and they'd hardly do him any good now they've shrunk with us, would they? And..."—she seemed to consider it gravely—"...the food!" She smiled and nodded at him. "Yes, I'm certain that's why! You said it yourself only a moment ago! We could have eaten a hundred of those berries at our proper size and probably would've needed to in order to quench our thirst! Not to mention those nuts we ate last night! We'd have wasted loads of time cracking enough to eat our fill!"

"That's true enough," he agreed. "I suppose it's as good a reason as any!" He picked up the sword and strapped the scabbard back in place. He made sure Alice didn't see him wince as he tightened it on his sore shoulders.

The grassy, downhill slope made the walk into the field of flowers almost leisurely compared to their rough rambling over roots and stems the day before, and Alice's exclamations became more and more ecstatic as they stepped in among the infinite sea of flowers. "It's just like I thought, Vincent. It's the loveliest place I've ever seen. Like strolling beneath thousands of blue parasols!"

"It is almost exactly like that." Vincent smiled.

"And the smell is nearly intoxicating!" She twirled and her tawny skirt spiraled out like a dusty sunflower. "I could stay here forever and not mind a bit!"

If only....

The further they went into the flowers, the less they talked. A hazy calm descended over him like a blanket.

It's something about this place—quite like walking through a daydream.

Endless stalks and endless blue lay before them. And the longer they walked, the less interested Vincent felt in anything at all. He became drowsy and his thoughts murky the way they always did when he sat in front of a warm fire on a cold evening.

A fire? What's that? My, what silly thoughts I'm having.

He looked around to see the figure of a girl melting into the expanse of flower stalks stretching ahead of him.

There's someone else here, I suppose. How interesting!

He whistled as he walked.

Why am I walking, though? I may as well sit down if I don't care to go anywhere else.

He leaned back into a nearby stem only to find something pressed into his back painfully. He straightened and reached behind himself.

"What's this? Something like a long stick, I think. And why is it stuck to my back?" He pulled, and it came free. "Ooh, it's very pretty," he said to no one. He held the sword in both hands and swung it in a circle, coming quite close to cutting off his own head. "*Swish, swish!*" he said aloud.

"Stop that infernal nonsense!" a voice called out from somewhere above Vincent's head. "Going to cut me in two! You can't just go around destroying mushrooms. Where would we be then? And keep your voice down!"

Vincent looked up.

"Why, hello, mushroom!"

"I didn't say I *was* a mushroom!" the voice called back.

Vincent squinted up at something like gills and remained completely unflustered. "You do look like a mushroom, though. Are you a sort of cousin to it?" He grew puzzled.

Only when have I seen a mushroom before?

"Don't be ridiculous." The voice broke Vincent's train of thought. "Mushrooms don't talk nor do their cousins." It continued muttering, but so quietly only a rush of terse whispers reached Vincent's ears.

"If you say so." Vincent shrugged. He began whistling again.

A wormy green and yellow head poked out between the frills. "Stop that absurd racket!"

"Oh! You're a caterpillar!" Vincent scrunched up his face, concentrating very hard. "Or perhaps I dreamed a thing called a caterpillar."

"I don't know about a caterpillar, but I AM a *first,* you know. Possibly one of the only firsts left, and I demand respect. I am in hiding, and you're going to attract a great deal of attention I'd rather not have if you continue to carry on like that. So, stay silent or go away."

"Hiding?" Vincent smiled wide. "Is it a game? I've an idea I like games."

The caterpillar withdrew back into the mushroom and called out, "Not a game!" then muttered, "Shouldn't even bother talking to them when they're like this."

"Talk to who? Are there others here, then? I think I saw a creature something like me earlier."

"Talk to any of them! You, included. Now, GO AWAY."

"But what are you hiding from?" Vincent asked again. "I've been here forever, and nothing bad has ever happened."

"Oh, bother!" The caterpillar reappeared with something in several of its hands and threw it.

It hit Vincent squarely on the top of his head and bounced off.

Vincent laughed and picked it up. "This is very springy. Is it part of your mushroom? I've a mind to climb on top and jump up and down. I think I would bounce right up several yards and land without hurting myself a bit!"

"Don't you dare, you imbecile. Now, eat that bit of mushroom I threw down!"

"Oh, it's a snack, then? Even better!" Vincent popped it into his mouth. He chewed and chewed, but it was quite tough and unpalatable. He came very near to spitting it out just as a thought struck him.

I haven't been here forever! What was I thinking?

And then another, more frantic.

Alice!

CHAPTER SIXTEEN

The heart of man is very much like the sea—it has its storms, it has its tides, and in its depths, it has its pearls, too.

—Vincent van Gogh

The sword dropped from his hand. He shook his head in an attempt to dispel the cobwebs.

"Good!" the caterpillar said. "Got your wits about you?"

"Yes! What happened? I've lost Alice?"

"Now you'll remember there's good reason for me to hide, and you'll get yourself away from this field as quickly as possible before the spell sets in again."

"What do you mean?" Vincent asked.

"The flowers! Everyone who steps foot in here goes mad. And this mushroom is the only antidote! Thought the word had gotten around, and I'd be rid of the dangers of mad passers-by like yourself. So, off you go."

"But how will I find my friend?" He nearly forgot about the tove. "And Duke, too! I've got to find them!"

"Not my problem, I'm sure." The caterpillar pulled his head back in.

"Think, Vincent, think." He paced back and forth beneath the mushroom. "All right, if the mushroom is the remedy, I must take some of it, find Alice and Duke, and give it to them as well. Then we can get out of this accursed place."

"Wouldn't do any good." The fronds of the mushroom muted the caterpillar's voice. "Got to be fresh. Its power fades in moments once you break it off."

"OK. Then I'll find them and get them out of the field."

The caterpillar reemerged, several pairs of its arms crossed in front of its body. "No good."

"And why not?" Vincent yelled.

It scowled in obvious annoyance. "I've said the mushroom is the only antidote, and even that won't work if the poison's been in the system too long. Becomes permanent, of course." It said this with maddening condescension.

A knot of despair tightened in Vincent's chest. "Permanent? How long till that happens?"

"Can't say. Depends on your species, what you've eaten, how big you are. The smaller you are, the less time it takes. I daresay at your size, you wouldn't have lasted much longer."

"Well, you might help me think of something since you know so much!" Vincent stalked away.

He hadn't gotten far when the voice called out. "Come back!"

He strode back, anxiously anticipating the caterpillar's advice.

The creature peered down at Vincent haughtily, but said nothing, so Vincent prodded. "Well? Did you want to say something?"

"Yes," it said.

"Go on, then!"

"Keep your temper." The derision in the caterpillar's voice sent hot blood rushing to Vincent's face.

"Is that all? You may lose your temper, too, if you'd lost your friends and may never get them back."

He stomped off again, determined to exert every ounce of energy in finding them, but the caterpillar called him back again.

Vincent whirled. "If you tell me to keep my temper again, I'll…."

"No, no. You were quite right, my boy. I know the fear of losing friends. There's only one way out of this. Find your friends and bring them back here, but don't take too long or your own antidote will wear off and you'll be right back in the same fix."

"How long till the mushroom wears off?"

The caterpillar threw him another bite. "Eat this, and then I'd say about a quarter of an hour."

"That's no time at all to search a field this size!" Vincent said. "Can't I eat more?"

"No. The mushroom has its own ill effects in large quantities. Trust me, I'd know."

Vincent ate his bite.

But how am I going to find them in this huge field?

He squinted his eyes to think, then opened them in sudden realization.

That's it! The field is huge, but I can be, too.

He stepped back from the mushroom and stuck his hand in his right pocket. He reached for cake, but his fist closed around something else—something he'd put out of his mind—the blindfold. He pulled it out along with his bite of cake.

No time to hesitate.

He put the blindfold on and ate a bite of the cake, growing quite large—as large as he dared. He scanned the field, eyes closed behind the blindfold. The blue cast of the flowers wafted and wavered in every direction, rising and flowing like a great river. He towered over them like a monstrous tree.

At first, he worried how he would find the mushroom again but noted a yellow gleam rising from it, faint even with his blindfold, but there. He'd be able to pick it out amidst all this rushing whirl of blue.

He searched for Alice's fiery shimmer. He almost called her name but remembered he hadn't cared about anything at all while under the influence of the flowers.

She wouldn't answer. Probably wouldn't even know her own name.

A pang of worry stabbed his heart.

What if I miss her? What if I trample her as I feared she would me when I was small? What if I don't find them in time?

But he tried to put all the awful possibilities from his mind. He had to act.

He strode swiftly, and his every move caused whirlpools of color to spin away from him like ribbons caught in the wind. He took some pleasure in smashing the enchanting flowers in his wake.

Dratted trickery to be so beautiful but so dangerous!

Even with his blindfold, the flowers gave no hint of their treacherous power.

I guess my vision has its limits.

He turned to the left and saw nothing but blue all the way to the edge of the wood. He looked to the right—nothing. He looked straight ahead and....

No, no, no! Not now!

A whirling shadow floated along the edge of the glen, as dark as the rabbit had been light.

CHAPTER SEVENTEEN

Many people seem to think it foolish to believe that the world could still change for the better. Yes, evil often seems to surpass good. But then, in spite of us, and without our permission, there comes at last an end to the bitter frosts. One morning the wind turns, and there is a thaw. And so, I must still have hope.

—Vincent van Gogh

Vincent's stomach clenched in horror. This was worse than he'd feared—a black, cavernous pit of malevolence swelling and constricting with vile breaths, exhaling an inky vortex of death and drinking away all the colors in its path. He could feel it reaching, grasping. It was hunting; it was going to kill.

He reached for the sword at his back and grasped only empty air. Then he remembered dropping it by the mushroom. He squeezed his eyes shut.

Think, think. Just get Alice. I have to find her.

He resolutely turned his back to the monstrosity. A brown and green swirl of strands rose just above the blue surface mere yards from where he stood. Not Alice, but Duke.

He desperately panned the field for a glimpse of Alice's amber glow but didn't find her. He wanted to scream but knew he couldn't leave Duke.

Alice would never forgive me.

He approached the earthy tendrils rising from the tove, and though Duke should have been visible at his natural size, Vincent had to stoop and part the flowers to see him. He lay sprawled on his back, lounging beneath the petals, flicking one with a careless paw. He seemed completely unafraid and undaunted but proved difficult to catch, nonetheless. Duke did not speak, but when Vincent reached for him, he rolled away in a sort of slithery tumble and let out an odd chitter.

Vincent scowled and grabbed again.

The beast is laughing at me!

This time Duke dove madly, burying himself amidst a particularly thick patch of flowers with that same maddening chuckle then gamboling and spinning about like a gyroscope.

"It's not a game, Duke," Vincent whispered, afraid his giant's voice would attract the Jabberwock's attention.

"'Tis, 'tis!" Duke tittered and attempted to roll again. "Quite fun. Catch me if you can!"

But this time Vincent did catch him, and the tove wriggled and writhed terribly in his grip.

"I do believe you're enjoying this!" Vincent struggled to keep his grip. "I'll drop you and then you'll see how fun it is! Now, be still!"

"Won't! Try and make me!" Duke chittered and roiled in his hand.

Vincent did drop him from the height of a few feet once he reached the mushroom. "Give him a bite quickly. He's more beast-like than ever."

The caterpillar threw down a piece of the mushroom.

"Eat it, you little idiot," Vincent said and immediately felt bad about it, but worry for Alice consumed him, and Duke's behavior was just slowing him down.

Thankfully, the tove needed no further encouragement and devoured the mushroom in seconds. Vincent watched its reason return in stages.

"Oh! I think I've acted a bit foolish even for a tove!"

"Don't worry about that now," Vincent said, glancing regretfully at the fallen sword. But he hadn't been wearing it when he changed sizes.

I'll need more than a two-inch blade to inflict a mortal wound.

He sighed. "I've got to find Alice, Duke. You just stay here, and don't wander off!"

He stood from his crouch, fearing all the while that evil lurked at his back. He turned a full circle but saw nothing.

Maybe it's done its deed and moved on.

This thought held little comfort. If so, it had killed something. He had felt its need.

Just don't let it be Alice.

He shook himself.

If I don't find her fast, it won't matter if the beast gets her or not.

The poison would take her for good.

Vincent strode quickly opposite the direction he'd found Duke, focusing on every shimmer and nuance of color and light. He cast his eyes across the field all the way from his feet to its horizon. He finally glimpsed a ripple of red-orange and took off at a sprint.

When he reached it, he bent to find an apparently contented Alice smiling up at him between the flowers.

"My, but you're large!" she said. "I believe just one of your eyeballs is larger than my own head! I didn't know anyone could be so big! Is it uncomfortable?"

Vincent didn't try to reason with her. He simply scooped her up in one hand and took off for the mushroom.

"Oh!" she cried, giggling all the while. "What an adventure this is, though it took me by surprise! Nothing ever happened to me before, though I didn't mind at all. It was simply delightful where you found me, but this is wonderful, too." She chattered away, not even slightly concerned at flying through the air in the hand of a giant.

He reached the mushroom in minutes, watching for the Jabberwock all the while.

He did not drop Alice as he had the tove but placed her gently beside the mushroom.

"Caterpillar!" He forgot to lower his monstrous voice and winced at it echoed across the field. He raised his head to scan for that black abyss. He didn't dare take off the blindfold in case it showed up again. The caterpillar was right. They didn't need to attract attention, and Vincent's size already made him the most conspicuous thing around.

He parted the flowers and whispered this time. "What are you waiting for, Caterpillar? Give her some of the mushroom!"

A piece fell on the ground next to Alice, and she plopped down next to it, then picked it up and squeezed it. "What's this? It's very squishy."

"Eat it," the caterpillar said.

She looked up, wide-eyed and cheery. "Hello! Who are you?"

The caterpillar harrumphed. "I am a *first*. I might ask who you are!"

Alice's face grew puzzled. "I suppose you might, but now you mention it, I'm not sure I know." She peered at Duke. "Do you know who I am?"

"Yes, miss. You're Alice, and a very kind lady."

"Oh, that sounds lovely," Alice smiled.

"Now, you should eat that squishy stuff you're holding, miss," Duke said.

"Certainly!" she said and ate it with no hesitation whatsoever.

Vincent watched as her face passed from delight to concern and, finally, to alarm.

"What happened?" She looked up and screamed when she saw Vincent's great face hovering above her head. "What were we thinking? We've wasted half the day!"

"Don't worry about that," Vincent said. "It's the flowers; they're a poison of some sort and that mushroom is the cure, so we're all right for the moment." He addressed the caterpillar. "What of the time? Is it safe for me to take another bite so I don't lose myself again?"

"One more shouldn't hurt since a few minutes have passed," the voice called from beneath the mushroom. "But not at that size or it'll do you no good at all! You'd need to eat the whole mushroom at your height, and I'll not have that! And keep it down, for my sake if not your own!"

"Right!" Vincent grabbed a vial of tea from his pocket and swigged it. He grabbed the sword first thing, heaving a sigh of relief, then gobbled a bite of the mushroom.

The caterpillar spoke again. "Now that your reason is restored, I'll thank you to leave me in peace. You've undoubtedly alerted every monster in the vicinity, and I probably won't last the night, but I'll not give in easily. I am one of the only firsts left, and that terrible creature loves the firsts, you know. You'll want to head that way."

Vincent's blood curdled as several pairs of its arms pointed in the direction he'd seen the Jabberwock.

The caterpillar continued talking. "You will come out of the field at a creek. Follow it downstream, and do it quickly before the madness sets in again."

"I'm terribly sorry, caterpillar." Alice furrowed her brow. "It must be very frightening to be a first. We didn't mean to frighten you more."

"Frighten me?" It sounded indignant. "As if a trifling little thing like you could do anything to frighten someone like me."

"Trifling? Why, if I was at my right size…." She straightened her dress as if that would settle her temper. "Three inches is such a wretched height."

"I am EXACTLY three inches high, thank you very much, and it's a very good height indeed!" the caterpillar yelled. "So very rude! I came here so no one could find me, not to have witless creatures imperiling my life. I've got posterity to think of! There will never be more firsts, after all. Must preserve myself. Now, go away!"

"Well, if that's your plan, there's not much of a point." Alice crossed her arms every bit as stubbornly as the caterpillar had earlier.

"And what do you mean by that?" the caterpillar asked.

"I'd rather not be safe if it meant living alone in that mushroom for the rest of my days! You may as well let the Jabberwock get you for all the good you can do in there."

"That's no business of yours!" It retreated within the mushroom's gills again.

"I beg your pardon!" Alice's face flushed.

"One shouldn't beg. It isn't respectable," the caterpillar yelled. "And, for the last time, go away!"

"Gladly!" Alice said. "Come, Vincent." She stamped away in a huff. "It's very keen to be on its own, and if we're going to fight the Jabberwock, we can't lose our minds in this wilderness of flowers again. I suppose we needed to talk to the caterpillar so we wouldn't sit in this field like mindless fools for the rest of our lives—which probably wouldn't have been long given how indifferent I'd become. I'm certain I'd have let myself starve to death! But I do wish the rabbit had set less provoking creatures in our path." She put a hand on Duke. "Except for you, dear. You're just perfect."

"Thank you, miss," Duke replied shyly.

"I thought you liked the cat," Vincent said.

"Well…"—she hesitated a bit—"…he could've been more pleasant. He did tell us the truth about the madness, though."

They had taken been marching in the direction the caterpillar had indicated when its voice rang out again. "Come back."

Vincent stopped.

"Leave it be, Vincent. It's made its position quite clear."

"He eventually said something useful when I couldn't think how to save the two of you," Vincent said. "I guess we ought to find out what he wants."

Alice shrugged and followed him back toward the mushroom.

"Did you say you were going to fight the Jabberwock?" The caterpillar asked as they approached, raising one eyebrow.

"Yes, and to kill it," Alice said.

"Hmm, quite confident, are you?"

Alice's voice didn't waver a bit. "Very confident, yes."

Vincent spoke up, too. "And we'd thank you not to be a naysayer."

"Fine and dandy for you to say!" The caterpillar snorted. "You're not a first!"

Vincent's temper rose again. "I'm sure a first is a very fine thing, but at least we aren't cowering beneath a mushroom. You're awfully fond of your pedigree, but if it doesn't give you any more dignity than that, it isn't worth much. We'll be on our way as you asked." He strode away once again. "Come on, Alice. I only wish we could get away from that caterpillar faster! It is quite provoking as you said."

"Definitely," Alice said. "Let's go back to our regular sizes. We would go faster then."

Vincent didn't want to do that in case the Jabberwock lingered.

Not sure I want to bring that up just now, though.

So, he said instead, "I'm afraid you were right, and I'm using up my tea and cakes rather too quickly. We'd probably better stay the size we are as long as possible."

"You could hop on my back," Duke said. "That'd be much quicker."

"I don't know," Vincent said.

Duke mistook the reason for Vincent's hesitation and said, "I'll be very gentle, sir."

"I know, Duke. I haven't any concerns about our safety in your hands, but I know from experience that hanging on to your fur is like wrestling a slippery goose. We'd fall off in a second!"

"That'll actually be easier at your size, sir. You'll just dig your hands as far into my fur as you can and then twist them like this." He demonstrated, rotating his little paws in the air. "It's as good as lashing you down."

"Thank you for the lesson, Duke," Alice said, "but won't that pull your fur terribly?"

"Oh, no, miss. No more than it should."

They climbed on Duke's back, following his instructions as to how to hang on. The tove ran as quickly as he could, and though happy for the speed, Vincent thought it very uncomfortable. Duke took long leaps, and the landings jarred him terribly.

Vincent also still wore the blindfold.

What if the Jabberwock comes back?

He searched the horizon for any signs of it. At Duke's speed, all the world flashed by like a kaleidoscope of fantastic light twisting and twirling around his head. He wished he could shut it off but didn't dare remove the blindfold. And as the murmur of rushing water reached his ears, shadows like smoky fingers also wavered in the distance—but not the Jabberwock itself.

Too indistinct for that.

The Jabberwock's victim lay ahead. He didn't mention it to the others. What was there to say?

CHAPTER EIGHTEEN

The fishermen know that the sea is dangerous and the storm terrible, but they have never found these dangers sufficient reason for remaining ashore.

—Vincent van Gogh

The flowers thinned as they drew nearer the creek, and they finally exited them altogether upon reaching the sandy bank beside the stream. A terrible sight greeted them.

Ten or twelve little shells lay on the sandy shore, open but intact, dark tendrils of death rising from them in Vincent's altered sight, their insides reduced to little more than dust. The small corpse they'd seen earlier had been horrifying, but this scene was worse because one—and only one—little oyster remained alive, shuddering on the bank.

Guilt washed over Vincent like a sickening wave.

Could I have prevented this? But I…I couldn't…I had to get Alice.

Alice's eyes filled with tears, and she hid her face in Duke's fur. "The poor dears! They're all shriveled up."

But when a tiny sob sounded, she raised her head.

The lone surviving oyster lay weeping beside the others.

Alice appeared to have some trouble untangling her hands from Duke's fur, as did Vincent, but she freed herself first. By the time he joined her, she already knelt beside the miserable oyster, resting one hand on its shell.

Vincent turned away, hardly able to bear its sorrow, which churned around it like the palest blue-gray smoke. The sorrow did not waft and rise as the colors normally did but crept sluggishly along the ground, surrounding the little creature in a cloud.

"Are you all right, dear?" Alice finally asked.

It snorted and choked in a very oystery fashion. "I'm the only one left." It sniffed. "It got the first already and…and…these were the youngest! It only left me because I'm the eldest and it said…"—the oyster gave a sort of a honk—"…said I'd be too stale and thin." It gave a whistling wail, and the air around it shimmered with a faint black trail. "I hate it!" it shouted.

When the oyster yelled, a tiny version of that evil mass Vincent had seen suddenly manifested all around it, causing Alice's light to dim as well. Vincent ripped off the blindfold.

I can't watch anymore! I don't want to see!

Duke let out a little snuffling sob. "I'm sorry. I've held it in, but, you know, there was another tove—the first—and it was my...my...."

"Oh, Duke!" Alice left the oyster's side and put her hand on Duke's back. "I'm so sorry. I didn't realize...." Alice's face paled, and she looked at Vincent. "The little creature we saw the first day...." She put her hand across her mouth as if to hold in a cry.

Vincent tightened his jaw. He pictured that first little mummified body and had no doubt she was right.

And he was doubly glad he'd taken off his blindfold, because even in his regular sight, Alice's expression pained him. Her face, normally sunny and joyful, was now gray and fearful, dull and downhearted. He closed his eyes, glad he could still shut things out.

I can't stand it. That little oyster!

Darkness had distorted it into something coal-black and unrecognizable. Vincent understood now. He understood all too well.

The Jabberwock stole time, yes. But it also spread itself to those it encountered in its path of destruction.

I don't want this sight! I don't want it!

Vincent pictured his own world.

How many people lived enshrouded in that black horror? Or what if people's color just fades away?

He visualized Alice's brilliant colors—washed-out when they'd become lost, dimmed and diluted as she sat beside the oyster. Hers had returned quickly, but what if some people's color paled altogether, never to return? He thought of his mother. Could she be so careworn and tired that not a spark of her color was left?

I couldn't bear it!

He suddenly realized Alice was shaking him.

"Vincent! We have to go."

She stood back and observed the oysters once more. She shivered then tossed her hair over one shoulder, determination evident on her face.

"We've got to get it, Vincent. Before it kills any more creatures and leaves them like this. I said earlier I didn't really want to find it. Now, I do. No matter how horrible it is."

She's found her focus just as I've lost mine.

Alice looked at him. "The caterpillar said to go downstream, and I know just how to do it. And fast."

He said nothing but stood and followed Alice's lead.

She climbed onto Duke's back, and he climbed up behind her, not even paying attention to where they went until the shock of a cold wave doused his body. He gasped, inhaling a large mouthful of water as he realized they'd entered the stream. Duke swam along with the current.

Vincent closed his eyes.

I can't bear this sight if it's going to show me what people have lost, how it changes them....

And then his eyes popped open.

Alice was shaking me, and my vision didn't change.

He unwound one hand from Duke's fur and reached forward, tentatively placing it on Alice's shoulder. She smiled back at him. He returned the smile as if his only purpose had been reassurance. The thunderous creek prevented conversation and opening his mouth at all was likely to result in swallowing a great gulp of water, so he didn't speak.

Nothing. Everything's normal!

He removed his hand and attempted to evaluate if the bleary edges in his regular sight had resolved, but with the water constantly splashing in his face, he couldn't properly test it.

He closed his eyes again—a nagging fear settling in his gut. The rabbit's words came back to him: *"Practice your gifts…the stronger they are, the better your chances…."*

Then we're all doomed because my gift is gone altogether.

CHAPTER NINETEEN

Right now, it seems that things are going very badly for me, have been doing so for some considerable time, and may continue to do so well into the future. But it is possible that everything will get better after it has all seemed to go wrong. I am not counting on it. It may never happen, but if there should be a change for the better, I should regard that as a gain. I should rejoice. I should say,

'At last! So, there was something after all!'

—Vincent van Gogh

They rode on and on, never drying though they sat above the water level on Duke's back. Tiny rapids and waterfalls dotted the stream, splashing them at every turn. Eventually, Alice reached back and placed a hand on Vincent's shoulder.

Finding our way, I suppose.

Alice yelled something unintelligible, and a moment later, Duke veered toward the bank and ambled over the rocky shallows.

When they reached the shore, Vincent rolled off Duke's back and landed squarely on the sword.

"Ow," he groaned. He removed it and rolled onto his back, immensely grateful for the dry ground beneath him. Alice seemed to feel the same, sitting in the sand next to him and stretching her back. Duke wandered off into the trees on some unknown errand.

Vincent stared up through the treetops, squinted, and tried to focus, but the leaves still melded together fuzzily. The lines of the trunks blurred ever so slightly into the surrounding sky.

So...regular sight is altered forever, I guess.

He closed his eyes again.

I don't have the energy to think about that right now.

He squeezed and released his fists alternately. "Whatever Duke said, hanging on that way is tough on the hands."

"Indeed," Alice said, taking turns massaging one of her own with the other. "One can't help but clinging as if your life depended on it, and, at our size, in those rapids, it probably did!"

"Yes, probably so."

"How are you getting on?" a voice rang out as loud as a foghorn.

Alice gasped sharply, and Vincent sat up, reaching for the sword before the swish of an enormous, striped tail told him all he needed to know. The Cheshire cat lounged on a fallen tree and dwarfed them at their current size.

That thing could kill me with one swipe.

The sword wouldn't do any more harm than a large thorn at their current size.

"Cheshire cat," he called, "you certainly make a habit of appearing out of nowhere."

"That's what cats do, you know," Alice said.

"Well, it's not polite to sneak up on people," Vincent said.

"I'm not sneaking," it said. "If your ears are so useless they can't hear one walking, one can hardly be blamed. Or would you like it if I wore a little bell 'round my neck like her Dinah?"

"I'm certainly in favor if you're going to keep showing up like that," Vincent replied.

"Vincent!" Alice scolded. "You need to work on your greetings."

He shrugged. "My greetings are perfectly satisfactory if I actually want to see someone."

"Hello, Cheshire Cat!" Alice called up cheerily. "I do apologize for Vincent. He's unnecessarily cross with you."

The cat grinned but said nothing.

"Though I have to admit," she whispered to Vincent, "I'm afraid even my Dinah might eat me if she met me at this size."

"I shan't eat you yet, my dear. There are tastier things in the forest, and besides, I like to tease my food a bit first."

"I didn't mean to imply…" Alice said. "You do have very good ears, don't you?"

It grinned at them terribly. "I find your size somewhat curious. You were larger before, yes?"

"Oh, yes! It's very curious, indeed!" Alice said.

Vincent spoke before she could continue. "Odd world you have here; strange things keep happening. We never know what to expect!" He didn't want to tell it about the rabbit any more than he'd wanted it to know about Duke.

"Hmm," it said.

"And you were so right about the madness," Alice said. "If we hadn't found…."

Vincent broke in. "Yeah, if we hadn't found that mushroom, we never would've escaped. Lucky break I was hungry, really."

"Yes…lucky," the cat said.

Alice looked at Vincent quizzically. He didn't speak and could feel the cat's eyes boring into him.

"You're soaked through, though," it said, voice dripping with sympathy. "Tell me you didn't come down the river."

"We did, though," Alice said. "It was dreadfully exciting!"

"Yes," Vincent interrupted again. "Thought we'd drown or be pounded to death by rocks in the stream, but we made it somehow."

"Indeed." The cat droned on in a bored, monotonous tone. "I'm sure you'll manage the stinging things as well then."

"Stinging things?" Alice jumped to her feet for the first time since rolling off Duke's back. "Is that where we are?"

"I'm afraid so. Good luck to you." The cat sauntered away without another word.

Vincent shushed Alice when she began to speak.

"Don't shush me!" she said. "I let you do it with the cat around because I guessed you may have your reasons, but I'll not let you do it now!"

"Calm down, Alice!" he said, once confident the cat was out of earshot. "I only didn't want it to hear anything we might say."

"I still say you're overreacting. What if it is one of the animals that's supposed to help us on our way? How can it if you won't tell it anything?"

"I don't trust it! It said it liked to tease its food, and I think that's just what it was doing to us!"

"You haven't doubted any of the other creatures we've met!" Alice said.

"None of them have said anything about eating us!"

"That was just a little joke because of what I said about Dinah!"

"Maybe," Vincent said. "But you're too trusting, Alice."

"Well, you're not trusting enough. And you seem happy enough I trust you!"

Vincent sighed and closed his eyes. "I'm sorry. Let's just forget about it."

"Very well." Alice nodded curtly and began strolling around their little cove.

Vincent sat back down on the shore, weary and out of sorts from their disagreement.

"My, but the trees are large, aren't they?" Alice said.

Vincent's concentration had been on his sight at first and the cat next. The size of the trees hadn't even registered. "They are big…but perhaps they just seem so because we're still so small."

"No, these are far beyond that! The trees in the other forest look like little weeds compared to these!" Alice turned in a circle.

Vincent stood to get a better sense of his surroundings. "Yes, I think you're right."

A rustling noise from behind startled him, and Vincent rounded to see the caterpillar. It spoke a pompous, "Ahem, ahem," using the actual word, then peered off into the distance, awaiting their acknowledgement.

Vincent glared at it. "I wish everyone would announce themselves properly and stop creeping out from the shadows. What are you doing here?"

"Not a very agreeable welcome, if I do say so myself," the caterpillar replied. "Where are your manners, boy?"

"According to my mother, I lost them in the creek," Vincent said.

"No." The caterpillar cast his eyes down and held several hands up. "I'm afraid it's me who should apologize."

"I wasn't apologizing," Vincent said. "And how did you get here so fast? There's no way you can crawl as fast as Duke swam down that stream."

"Silk—you know, riding the winds through the trees. Quite invigorating. Haven't done it in ages."

"I'm so glad you enjoyed your trip." Vincent flexed his tired hands and suddenly felt very resentful of his wet clothes.

"Thank you, young master." The caterpillar actually bowed this time. "And not only for your well-wishes, but for calling me to task. I shall go with you. It is my duty." His antennae twitched as he wiggled his nose.

"You're welcome," Vincent grumbled.

I rather wish I'd kept my mouth shut.

"You were right, my boy. Nobility such as I shouldn't be more cowardly than the nobodies of the world." He crawled up beside them and continued in his blustering manner. "I'm ready to embark upon my worthy quest." It prattled on saying nothing of any importance with a great many words as Alice and Vincent both watched.

"He is absolutely infuriating," Alice whispered to Vincent.

"Yes, well, I suppose we'll just have to put up with him." He paused. "I wish we were our right sizes."

Alice giggled. "Imagine if we were! The caterpillar would only be as big as a finger. He wouldn't seem so imperious then!"

It finally finished its speech, never realizing they weren't listening at all, and looked at them expectantly.

Vincent inhaled deeply. "Glad to have another on our side." He reached out to shake the caterpillar's hand but found the etiquette of shaking the hand of something with so many feet far exceeded his capabilities. He grabbed the one furthest extended, but the caterpillar yanked it back.

"What are you grabbing my foot for?" He dusted it off with another as if removing any germs Vincent may have left behind. "You're an odd creature, aren't you?" The caterpillar sneered at him.

Vincent shook his head and changed the subject. "Well, what do you think about these astonishingly large trees, anyway? Alice and I were just discussing them."

"Nothing astonishing about it," the caterpillar said. "These are the big lands. Everything grows bigger here. I used to live here, you know; should've grown fifty times my size if I'd stayed."

"Really?" Vincent pictured a twelve-foot-tall caterpillar and didn't enjoyed the result. "So, when you say *everything's* bigger here, you mean…."

"Everything."

"That could become difficult, depending on the sorts of creatures about." Vincent glanced at Alice.

"Perfectly safe," the caterpillar said.

"But why is everything bigger?" Alice asked.

"How should I know?" the caterpillar said. "It just is. Why are you the size you are?"

Alice stared at the caterpillar blankly and seemed unable to think of a response to this. She promptly changed the subject. "Well, since you used to live here, could you find us some food?"

"Certainly. I can show you all the finest local cuisine."

"Good thinking, Alice," Vincent said, "and let's stay here for the night. The light is beginning to fade, and it's been a very trying day."

"That's certainly true," Alice said. "Losing one's mind is extremely demanding, I think."

"Not to mention swimming for hours with two creatures on your back!" Duke ambled back from wherever he'd gone.

"Indeed!" Alice put a hand on his head. "You deserve a good long rest! I'll go back to my right size and take the caterpillar to forage. If that's all right with you, caterpillar?"

"Ready to do my duty!" It saluted her.

"You don't mind going alone, Alice?" Vincent asked.

"She won't be alone for a second!" the caterpillar said, puffing out its chest. "I'll not desert a lady!"

Vincent ignored it.

"No, I don't mind going at all," Alice said. "You had a terrible time, too, what with having to chase me and

Duke down in that field. I'm sure it was awful, coming to your senses all alone!"

Vincent lay back on the shore, happy to rest for a few more minutes.

Alice ate a few bites of cake, growing steadily taller, then reached for the caterpillar. She hesitated before picking it up. "Is it all right?"

"As long as you're gentle," it said, "and mind the antennae."

"Certainly."

Alice placed him gently on her shoulder, and they strolled away.

The caterpillar began a lecture. "Now, my dear, if you do come across the Jabberwock, you'll want to look as old and insignificant as possible. The first is tricky as I believe age is hard to fake, but as you're already quite common, the second shouldn't be too difficult."

Vincent grinned at Alice's reply. She completely ignored the caterpillar's speech. "What shall we call you then, caterpillar?" she said. "You must have a name if you're to go with us."

As her words faded away, Vincent retreated into his thoughts and couldn't help but be disheartened by…well, everything when he stopped to think about it.

So far, they'd lost their way, fallen under the spell of poison flowers, encountered a dubious cat, and now they were stuck with that maddening caterpillar.

And I've lost my gift, too. The one thing we really need.

He thought of the withered oysters and Duke's... Duke's what?

Mate, probably. Could I have prevented the oysters at least? But how could I without the sword? And Alice! She might have forgotten everything...forever!

He closed his eyes, relaxing in the silence that fell over him. It didn't last long.

Mere moments later, Alice's footsteps roused him, thunderous at her great height and approaching rapidly.

Now what?

CHAPTER TWENTY

The more I think about it, the more I realize there is nothing more artistic than to love others.

—Vincent van Gogh

Vincent sat up and rushed to eat enough cake to approximate his proper height.

Three inches isn't a great height for emergencies.

He remembered the sword at the last minute, scrambling for it just in time.

Alice approached in a full sprint and nearly bowled him over.

"Calm down!" the caterpillar yelled. "Stop this indecorous retreat! What is the matter with you?"

"Alice!" Vincent said. "What's wrong?"

"The bees, Vincent! I've never imagined the like! They're humongous! As big as a cart horse, and their proboscises are the size of an elephant's trunk!"

"Their probo-whats?"

"You know! The thing they use to get the nectar! That's not the point, Vincent. Giant bees! They fly so clumsily just like bumblebees only they're ever so much larger! They're like...like...bumblephants or elebees. Oh, we can't stay here. There are thousands of them."

She said all this in a mad rush, the caterpillar attempting to speak over her the entire time. She finally stopped, clearly winded from her mad dash and her frantic speech, and the caterpillar's words became clear.

"Perfectly harmless! All this fuss! Great cowards! I suppose I should have known. Putting myself at risk. Might show some courage yourself!"

"Perfectly harmless, my foot!" Alice stamped like a toddler. "How do you know?"

"I lived among them, I told you! Splendid place for a caterpillar to live, among the bees. They work wonders for the vegetation."

"Then what are those enormous stingers for?" She didn't give the caterpillar a chance to answer before turning to Vincent. "See! Another thing the cat warned us about: 'stinging things with giant wings,' it said. It was telling the truth."

"Whoever told you that is most certainly untrustworthy!" the caterpillar insisted. "Those bees wouldn't hurt a...well...a caterpillar, I tell you."

"All right, all right!" Vincent said, holding up both hands and hoping for a truce. "This is getting us nowhere." He looked at the caterpillar. "Alice has a point. What are the stingers for if they aren't dangerous?"

"For defense, obviously!"

"And how do you know they won't think we're a threat and defend themselves against us?"

"They wouldn't care about you in the slightest! Only care about the great bird."

"Vincent!" Alice cried. "If there's a bird large enough to scare those monstrous things, it must be the size of London!"

"It is…ah…very sizable," the caterpillar admitted. "If there's anything to fear in this dale, it's that bird and not the bees. It swallows up ten of them in a bite."

"Ten of them?" Alice yelled. "Vincent! I tell you they're as big as horses!"

"Yes," Vincent said. "I'm not sure that makes me feel better. How often does this bird come around?"

"Only once a week or so," the caterpillar said.

"And is there a way to tell how recently it's come?"

"Not that I'm aware of, no."

Alice was still frantic. "We simply can't stay here, Vincent!"

Vincent put a hand on her arm to calm her and noted that his vision still did not engage when he touched her. He shrugged it off. "Your finding led us here, right, Alice?"

"Yes, but Vincent, it also led us into that terrible field where we almost certainly would have died if only from lack of caring."

"But it led us right, Alice. I saw…it."

Her eyes grew wide. "You saw what?"

"IT. The Jabberwock. While I was searching for you, I saw it on the edge of the clearing. I…I knew it was going to kill something, but I couldn't go after it because I didn't have the sword. I couldn't have risked you anyway, but the point is, you didn't lead us astray, and if we're going to face the Jabberwock, we may as well get some practice facing our fears."

I'm one to talk. I'm happy my vision is malfunctioning.

He took a deep breath. "We're here for a reason. So, I'll go with the caterpillar. You stay here and keep Duke company."

She nodded, a little shamefaced. "I'm sorry, Vincent. It's just…bees of all things. If it were anything else…."

He grinned. "I get it. If I didn't spend half my time out on the moor watching them, I may feel the same, but I've had them land on my nose and behave themselves in a perfectly respectful manner. Don't worry."

She shuddered. "Should one of these land on your nose, it would crush you to death!"

"I'm sure that won't happen." He transferred the caterpillar to his own shoulder.

"Gently, gently now," the caterpillar reminded him.

"Oh, I wouldn't think of endangering your highness!" Vincent said.

The caterpillar missed the sarcasm altogether and pointed officiously. "This way, my boy."

Vincent strolled off.

The daylight dwindled as he came to the top of a hill. A field much larger than the one with the unlucky blue flowers lay before him. This one held beautiful, variegated flowers nearly the size of trees, but that was hardly the most spectacular sight. Thousands of bee-like insects, three times Vincent's size, flew clumsily about the field.

"My, but they are daunting!" he said to the caterpillar. "If I hadn't prepared myself, I'd have run away, too. As it is, I daren't step foot among them."

"I suppose it would be only natural," the caterpillar admitted. "Should you have come along at your current height, I'd never have spoken a word." He pointed again. "Now, off we go."

Vincent followed the directions, grateful they skirted the edge of the field and that he needn't walk through all those giant bees. They approached a massive tree with a hollow inside.

"This is the biggest tree I've ever seen!" Vincent could have lain down inside of it, head to toe, ten times over.

"And full of honeycomb." The caterpillar rubbed several pairs of its hands together. "My favorite. Haven't had it in ages."

"I do love honey," Vincent said, "though I've never eaten it for a meal."

"Not the honey!" The caterpillar grimaced. "Nasty, sweet stuff. I'm after the comb."

Vincent wrinkled his nose. "Well, how about you take the comb and we'll eat the honey?"

"As you wish." The caterpillar grunted. "No accounting for tastes."

Vincent hesitated as he put one foot into the hollow. "Won't the bees attack if we take their honey?"

"Not at all! I'm telling you, they're the gentlest beasts, and can't you see there are none about anyway?"

"Yes. Just making sure. In our country, they'd likely swarm you and sting you to death if you tried, and they're much smaller than your kind."

"Sounds like they need to learn some manners then."

"I suppose you can hardly blame them minding someone stealing what they've worked hard to make."

I'm discussing the morality of bees with a caterpillar.

Vincent shook his head. "Never mind. In, I go." He stepped inside and could barely comprehend the height of this towering structure. The tree stretched up and up, hollow all the way to the top. Only a tiny pinprick of the deepening sky shone through the hole at the top. It might be miles away. And Vincent could have easily taken up residence in just one of the holes of the gigantic honeycomb, which lined every inch of the hollow tree all the way to the top.

"I think I'll shape a bit of the comb into a sort of bowl, then fill it with as much honey as I can carry," Vincent said. He pulled at the side of one empty comb and found it surprisingly pliable. He pulled off bits, molded them into a sort of bowl, then realized he could reshape the bowl after filling it, turning the container into something more like a jar for easier transport. It was sticky work, though. Honey trickled down his arms, and he spilled some down his back, gluing his shirt to his skin.

I'll have to take a thorough dip in that stream. And I'm only just now starting to dry!

He licked his fingers to get a taste.

"Oh, this is good!"

The caterpillar shook his head. "Syrupy, cloying taste."

Vincent found he'd made the jar too large once he brought it out through the opening. "I'll never be able to carry it the whole way."

"Just close up the end there, and roll it along," the caterpillar said.

"That might work. It's so thick; I don't think it would break." He evaluated the moss-covered ground ahead. "Maybe I won't go over anything sharp enough to pierce it."

This method worked splendidly, and he rolled it on back to their little spot beside the creek.

"What is it?" Alice asked. "Some sort of fruit?"

"No!" Vincent grinned. "It's honey! All closed up into the wax."

Duke licked his lips. "Mmm, honey is my favorite. Even better than the sweets you gave me, miss!"

"It's from those monstrous bees, I suppose," Alice said.

"Yes, but I'm practically covered in it, and I can tell you from experience, it's the best honey I've ever tasted."

"Hmm," Alice said. "You were right about the dramberries anyway, and I suppose I haven't a choice if I don't want to starve."

Vincent stood the jar on end and ripped a hole open in the top. He pulled off a chunk of comb as big as his head and passed it to the caterpillar.

"I suppose this is what you want."

"Indubitably!" It fell to with frightening rapidity.

"I almost forgot to tell you, Vincent,"—Alice mumbled through a mouthful of honey—"I've named the caterpillar."

"Oh, good. What are we to call his majesty?" Vincent said.

"Funny you should put it just that way." Alice smiled. "I've called him Cyrus. My sister was just reading from a book about Cyrus the Great…."

Vincent glanced at the caterpillar, who seemed preoccupied by his bit of honeycomb. "Whatever you do, don't say 'Cyrus the Great' where he can hear you!" he whispered.

"Indeed!" she grinned. "I wouldn't dare. Only he thinks so much of himself, he's quite as superior as Cyrus the Great!"

"That's the truth!" Vincent said.

It wasn't long before Alice lay back and groaned. "The honey is delicious, but I'm not certain a meal of it is advisable. One more bite, and I'm sure I would be sick."

Vincent agreed.

Duke, however, had downed roughly twenty handfuls of honey already and seemed remarkably revived. "Might I have the rest then?" he mumbled, his hand still in his mouth from the last bite.

"You do have a sweet tooth, don't you?" Alice laughed. "Eat as much as you like!"

At these words, the little tove put aside all pretense at composure, stood on its hind legs and stuck its whole face into the honeycomb jar, guzzling it in noisy slurps.

Alice wrinkled her nose and whispered. "He's very sweet but not quite civilized, is he?"

Vincent chuckled. "I suppose we can hardly expect it. He's not even supposed to be able to talk, is he?"

"That's true." She frowned. "I hope he can always talk while we're here. It would be sad for him to go back to being only a beast."

"Yes, I suppose it would be, but I think we'll be back home before that happens."

"Perhaps. But that will be a little sad, too, won't it?"

A cloud passed over Vincent's mind. "Yes. Will we ever see each other again? Once we go home, I mean."

"Oh, let's!" Alice put a hand on his arm. "We should plan it now. Anything may happen here, so we'd better set it all up. I suppose we couldn't manage it until we're grown, so what about when I turn twenty-one? I'm sure I could arrange a trip to Paris for my birthday, and we could meet at...at the Arc de Triomphe!"

"Perfect! When's your birthday then?" Vincent asked, somewhat uncertain he'd be able to manage the trip himself.

Mother and Father aren't exactly made of money.

"My twenty-first will be May the fourth, 1873," Alice said.

"I'll be there!" He jumped up. "Now, I'm going to wash in the creek before it gets any darker. I'm covered in honey, and I'd rather not sleep this way."

The fading sun already gave little enough light for this endeavor. He bathed quickly and returned to shore, pleasantly surprised at the effectiveness of his bath.

The tove lay nearby in a deep sleep, and the caterpillar was nowhere in sight. Alice lounged against an enormous tree trunk, feet propped on a mossy patch in front of her.

He shook his curly hair out then tried to smooth it down. "I'm glad it's not cold, anyway."

"Definitely," she replied. "Everything seems worse if you can't stay warm."

Vincent peeked into what remained of the honey bowl. "Duke did eat an impossible ration, didn't he? It's nearly gone!"

"I know." Alice giggled. "You should have seen him after he'd had his fill—as happy as a clam." Her face grew solemn. "Though I suppose the clams might not be any happier than the oysters around here."

Vincent sighed.

I guess I should tell her.

CHAPTER TWENTY-ONE

There may be a great fire in our soul, yet no one ever comes to warm himself at it, and the passers-by see only a wisp of smoke.

—Vincent van Gogh

"Alice, I seem to have lost my sight."

"Vincent!" He could only just see the concern on her face in the purple twilight. "Are you sure?" She stuck her hand out. "Take my hand and tell me what you see."

He took it.

Nothing.

He shook his head.

"Put on the blindfold then."

"Alice…."

"You've got to try! The rabbit said we needed to practice and that the stronger our gifts grew, the better our chances! How can you practice if it's not even working?"

He took a deep breath. "OK." He pulled the blindfold out of his pocket and put it over his eyes. He knew immediately it wouldn't work but let it play out for Alice's sake.

"Now, give me your hand again," she said.

Vincent reached out, and a warm hand met his own. The nothing that lay behind the blindfold felt safe. Easy. Normal.

Try, Vincent.

But it was no use. He didn't want to see. Not after the oyster. The rabbit told them to be decisive—resolute.

Well, I am…just in the wrong way.

Every time he tried to use his sight, that little oyster turned black with rage in his mind's eye.

"There's nothing, Alice."

"But, why, Vincent? I thought you'd begun to recognize the beauty in it."

"I had, but…."

"But what?"

"Then I saw the ugliness, too." He took the blindfold off, though it made little difference as full darkness had almost overtaken them.

Alice spoke softly. "What did you see?"

"The Jabberwock—not in its feeding form, I think; just as it is when it's invisible to everyone else. And that was bad enough. It was like looking into a pit of hatred. But my sight didn't go away then. Not until the oyster…."

Alice still held his hand, and she squeezed it when he said this. "I know. They were awfully sad, weren't they?"

"No, not the dead ones. I mean, they weren't pleasant either, but I'm talking about the one that was still alive." He paused.

"Oh?" Alice prompted him.

"Do you remember when it yelled?" he asked.

"Yes."

He shuddered. "I still wore the blindfold, and as it shouted, it turned all black and somehow hollow as if the Jabberwock itself leaked into the oyster. And that's just what did happen; I know it. It was helpless and angry, and the Jabberwock infects anything it touches with a little piece of itself. I think they begin to steal their own time from the inside. Unless they're very special...like Duke. Duke doesn't have a hint of it."

"But that's all the more reason to stop it, Vincent! It's horrid, but imagine how it will spread!"

"I know!" Vincent snapped at her. She did not release his hand. "But don't you see? The rabbit said our gifts would get as strong as we let them, and we'd be changed even in our own world. What if I go back and I find there's darkness in everyone? What if people there are empty and black? Or...when we got lost earlier, your colors faded. They came back, but what if they didn't? What if some people in our world are simply colorless because life took it all away? What about the people I love? How could I stand it?"

Alice clasped his hand between both of hers now. "But what if you could help those people who've lost their color or those who've let the darkness take over? And how reassuring it would be to see those who are still bright no matter what's happened to them! There are surely some of those."

He ignored her questions. "Promise me something, Alice."

"What?"

"I promised you I wouldn't become ordinary. I hope I can do it…even if my gift doesn't come back. But you promise me that you'll never fade. When I could still see your colors, they showed me why I'm at ease with you. You haven't let them spoil you and turn you into a little copy of everyone else, and you don't let things push you down."

She squeezed his hand again. "I…I think I can promise that. Especially now I know it's something real inside people that they can keep alive. It's not just an idea, but a real thing…part of themselves…and something that affects others, too."

"Yes!" he said. "That's it, exactly. And I'm afraid many don't manage it. When I think of the people I know… my family…." He paused for a long moment. "That's it, Alice. I'm afraid. Afraid to see people as they really are. And I can feel it, too. When that little oyster went black, it might've sent an arrow through my heart."

"But what about Duke?" she asked. "Shouldn't he give you hope? You said he's not affected."

"That's true. And…"—he grew a little shy—"you do, too. If everyone was like that, it would be delightful. But I'm afraid that's not how most people are. Just how we said—they're all shut up in their own heads and worried about things that don't matter and pretending to be the people they think everyone else wants them to be. I'm sure I will meet one sadness after another…or worse."

"You can't worry about that, Vincent. Think about what's in front of you today. Right now, if you haven't got your sight, we probably don't have a chance against the Jabberwock, and then all of this is likely not to matter at all because we'll be turned into mummies. Not to mention what will happen to this lovely world! It's only starting out! Think of all the loss already. We don't know how many aside from the oysters and Duke's mate and the little squirrel-like creature the rabbit showed us. Probably loads. The caterpillar itself said it's probably gotten all the 'firsts' it can find and moved on to the young ones. Think how awful, Vincent! The little…."

"I know, Alice!" Her speech only made him feel guiltier. "I'm trying! But deep down…"—he sighed—"… deep down, I just don't want it, and I can't make myself! I'm already different from everyone else, no matter how hard I attempt to disguise it. My family disapproves of me entirely unless I'm doing my very best to hide anything I actually feel or think or want, and I usually only manage to keep that up for a day or so. I'm not at all what my parents would have chosen for an eldest son. I don't have any friends. It's exhausting attempting to understand how to behave in front of people and pretending to care about silly things like clothes and being proper. It's just easier if I'm alone in my room or out on the moor for hours where

I don't have to pretend. The birds don't care if I'm respectable. But if I go back with this sight, it'll all be worse than it already is. I'll never be like other people."

"Vincent," Alice said gently, "I hope you never are. And didn't you just finish saying you were glad I wasn't like others?"

"Yes, but…"—he hesitated—"I've a feeling it isn't as hard for you. You're so happy and comfortable. I bet everybody loves you. I'm lucky to go an hour without upsetting someone."

"If you become like them," Alice said, "you'll only be doing just what you hate—letting them take all your color. If you did that, I think you'd be simply gray and miserable."

"But it's so hard not having anyone who understands you."

She squeezed his hand. "I don't think life is meant to be easy, but I think it's meant to be good…in the long run, if you can take it as it comes and do the best you can where you are."

And despite his discouragement, Vincent smiled and thought of meeting grown-up Alice in Paris, her colors still wild and vivid.

Would that pay for all in between?

"Just try, Vincent. We need to sleep now, but just try to want it…at least a little."

"I will, Alice. I promise."

Silence fell over them, and Vincent welcomed it like an old friend. Once again, Alice fell asleep in almost no time at all while Vincent lay awake for a very long while, staring at the nothing in the darkness above him.

The very peaceful nothing.

The rabbit's words came back to him. "*Practice your gifts.*"

Alice had worn her gloves faithfully from the moment she'd gotten them, but he'd barely touched the blindfold, afraid of losing his connection to the real world—a connection that hardly existed to begin with.

What am I even holding on to?

And what would it cost? All of Sian? Alice? Himself?

CHAPTER TWENTY-TWO

What preys on my mind is simply this one question: what am I good for? Could I not be of service or use in some way?

—Vincent van Gogh

Vincent woke in the early hours of the morning to a violent wind. The colossal trees creaked at each powerful gust, though Vincent would have said they stood too tall and anchored too deep for anything to shake them.

Alice's hair lashed her face like tiny whips as she surveyed the sky. "It can't be a storm, can it, Vincent?"

He scanned for clouds, but only the rising sun occupied the sky. "I don't think so. Is it?" He asked the caterpillar, who must have returned sometime after it grew dark the night before.

The caterpillar did not speak, but shook its head back and forth, trembling as it did so, its many feet clutching the fallen stick it sat on.

"There's a pattern in the wind," —Vincent's forehead wrinkled in thought—"like waves crashing and retreating...."—his eyes widened—"like wings."

Alice squinted at him in obvious confusion.

"Giant wings, Alice! It's the great bird! Come on!" He pulled her up with one hand, grabbed the sword in the other and ran, Duke hurtling along beside them. But Alice pulled him back.

"Cyrus!" She pointed.

Vincent looked back to see the caterpillar cowering where it stood. They dashed back, and Alice grabbed the stick he sat on.

"Hang on!" she yelled.

Darkness itself chased them as a vast shadow blocked out the sun. Then came the call, a shrieking, deafening din.

Vincent covered one ear with his free hand.

Leaves flew around their heads, and Vincent feared the massive trees would crash to the ground.

Alice suddenly stopped dead, yanking him to a standstill and nearly pulling him off his feet. She pointed at a deep hollow beneath a tree. "In here!" she shouted.

He couldn't think of a better option. A bird that size would catch them no matter how quickly they ran.

They dove into the shallow space and squished themselves in as far back as they could go. Alice squeezed his arm, and he put a hand on hers, but their eyes were riveted on the slice of sky still visible from their hollow.

Feathers as black as tar rippled overhead, blotting out every inch of the sun.

Something like a monstrous crow.

"Is it coming after us, you think?" Alice asked, her dark eyes mere inches from his.

"I don't know, but it's entirely too large to be safe, no matter what it's going after."

Duke sat between them, shuddering, and Vincent covered Cyrus with one hand, afraid the wind alone would blow him away.

The bird's shrill cry came again, nearer now.

"Vincent, look!" Alice cried.

Dread filled the pit of his stomach as a loathsome figure appeared. It didn't fly up behind the bird, didn't rise from beneath it. It simply materialized in the air.

The feeding form...

Vincent felt gutted.

I should have seen it coming.

"That's it, isn't it?" Alice said. "It's the Jabberwock, and it wants that bird."

Vincent nodded. "I've never seen it like this, but... the way it just appeared out of nothing like that...it has to be."

"But it's a...a..."

Alice didn't finish, so Vincent said it for her. "A dragon."

They sat frozen, eyes glued to the macabre scene.

The monster's long, green body glided through the air. It gave a rasping roar, and its leathery batwings beat relentlessly, fighting against the current of the great bird's flight. The Jabberwock's eyes gleamed, full of malicious fire. Its claws slashed as it neared the underbelly of the great bird. The bird flinched but didn't fall.

The bursts of wind continued, leaves spiraling frantically throughout the sky in a great cyclone. And then it happened.

The Jabberwock's razor talons caught hold of the bird, and cruel teeth closed around its neck. In mere seconds, the wind had stopped. The wings stiffened, then withered to nothing but ravaged skin and bone as its feathers disintegrated. The shadow cast by the bird thinned as the Jabberwock drained its time. An unnatural tranquility paralyzed the air itself, like the calm in the eye of a storm.

Then the Jabberwock vanished, and the corpse of the bird dropped from the sky like a ghastly devil.

"Hold on!" Vincent said. "It's going to be just like an earthquake when it hits!"

He thought of the Jabberwock.

"And stay hidden!"

What if it stays nearby? I can't see it until it turns into…into that monster. And what if that's too late?

Guilt struck him harder than ever, but he tried to assuage it.

No one else can see it either.

But he knew the truth.

Yes, and being just like everyone else is going to get us all killed.

He still held Alice's hand, and try as he might, no extraordinary vision came to him. How could he wish for that sight? He didn't even want to see the horror unfolding before him at this very moment.

What if the bird crashes where we sit?

Its carcass plummeted down and down, as big as a house, and finally hit in the field of flowers that had been buzzing with bees the day before. It did not stop where it landed but plowed through everything in its path, furrowing the ground for a hundred feet at least before coming to a stop. The quake caused by its landing reached them in waves. The tree they sheltered beneath leaned and creaked dangerously, but its roots held. The earth rumbled beneath them as if adjusting to this new weight settled upon it, and then all was silent and still.

A deadly calm.

Alice rose to a crouch and took a step out of their shelter, but Vincent pulled her back. "Not yet." He looked at the ground. "I can't see if it's gone." He leaned forward and drew the sword, grasping its hilt with both hands.

Alice did not scold him. She merely nodded and sat back down.

They waited for many minutes, no one speaking.

When the rustlings of other animals began, they finally exited the tree.

"Well," Cyrus said, "that was a near miss." He looked up at Vincent. "No thanks to you." The haughty accusation in his voice was unmistakable.

Vincent said nothing, not certain where this was coming from.

"I overheard your conversation last night," it said.

"Eavesdropping, were you?" Vincent didn't like its tone.

"It's hardly my fault you didn't hear my return." It gesticulated with its many arms. "And that's not the point. I gather you are resisting the very thing we need to kill this brute!"

"I…." Vincent shrugged. The caterpillar was right, and he felt disheartened and deflated, but…. "I don't want it, OK?" he burst out. "I can't make myself want something I don't want!"

"Selfish!" Cyrus said. "Only thinking of how it will affect you!"

"That's not fair," Alice said. "He's trying!"

But her defense only made him feel worse.

It's just like home. I can't do anything right, and I'm letting everyone down. Even the one person who believes in me.

CHAPTER TWENTY-THREE

If I am worth anything later, I am worth something now. For wheat is wheat even if people think it is a grass in the beginning.

—Vincent van Gogh

"Don't you say another word about it, Cyrus," Alice said. "Now, let's go. I suppose I found the Jabberwock this time as well, but it's probably moved on, so we should as well."

Vincent didn't look at her. He knew she didn't mean it as an accusation, but it felt like one.

She took his hand and put her other on the nearest tree. "So, let's find this thing, OK? It's going to work out. I know it." She smiled at him.

Vincent took a deep breath.

Maybe she's right. Maybe it will come out right in the end. She always makes me believe it might.

Alice found their way quickly, and they trudged off, the tove on her shoulders once again, the caterpillar on Vincent's, though not to the liking of either.

"You should put on the blindfold and try again," the caterpillar said.

"I'm telling you, I've tried, and with the blindfold on, all I'm going to do is stumble about and slow us down. I can't see a thing while I'm wearing it now."

"Then you should at least hold the girl's hand if that's supposed to strengthen this sight of yours. You should attempt it by any means possible! I daresay holding her hand won't cause you to stumble about."

"Fine!" Vincent grabbed Alice's hand. "Everything looks exactly the same. Are you happy?"

"Yes, actually." Cyrus nodded with satisfaction. "But with that attitude, it's definitely not going to work. Put your will into it, boy—a little determination! Some positive thinking!"

I'm going to put some will into flicking you into that tree in a minute.

"You said he'd be less imperious if he were only the size of a finger," Vincent grumbled to Alice.

The caterpillar snorted indignantly. Less than five minutes had passed when it asked, "Are you still trying to use your sight?"

"Yes!" Vincent yelled. "Yes, OK? And you're not helping. Of all the things I need, your pestering isn't one of them!"

"Just had to be certain. Can't count on everyone pulling their own weight."

"You're riding on my shoulder like some kind of royalty! Just how are you pulling your weight?"

"Of all the ungrateful..." the caterpillar started. "I did find you that honey, you know, and told you not to fear the bees. And you wouldn't have known about the bird...."

"OK, OK," Vincent said. "Just stop nagging me."

"As you wish!" Cyrus turned his head away. "I'll just sit here silently."

"Good," Vincent said.

"Good," the caterpillar echoed.

Vincent nearly screamed at it but decided it wasn't worth it.

Arrogant thing just wants the last word.

And he had it, for no one else dared speak for a very long while.

"Wish someone would find us some more honey," Alice said eventually, "or something to eat anyway."

"I could hop down and hunt a bit if you like, miss." Duke raised his head and searched out the air in every direction, whiskers wriggling. "Though I don't scent anything."

"Not yet, dear. I'm feeling more urgent all the time." Alice sighed.

But the landscape became increasingly difficult the further along they went. They'd left the big lands, crossing the river on a fallen tree. Few birds called out as they walked along, and thorny vines blocked them at every turn.

"There's just no reason for thorns this large!" Alice said crossly after one pierced her leg.

Between freeing themselves from the vines and attempting to avoid the veritable spikes, they made meager headway.

"We've been walking for hours," Vincent said.

"Yes." Alice frowned. "This is maybe the furthest we've gone without coming to something interesting except for when I got us lost."

"Maybe check our way again," he said.

She nodded and did so, shaking her head as if to clear it of cobwebs. "I think we're still going right."

"Then on we go." Vincent resumed their course immediately.

She smiled at him. "Thanks."

"For what?"

"For having confidence in me when I haven't got it in myself."

He shrugged. "I could say the same of you."

A glint of something caught Vincent's eye ahead—a shimmer that made him think, for just a moment, that his sight had come back. But when he focused on it, he recognized the familiar reflection of sun off the surface of a pond.

"Look, Alice!" He pointed ahead. "We may not have any food, but we can finally get a drink!"

She squinted through the trees. "I think you're right! I am thirsty!" Alice ran on ahead of him. "It is pretty," she called back. "I've never seen a pond so smooth."

Something nagged at the back of his mind—the image of the creek at home rose, its tiny currents circling out in all directions from insects and fish and the like. "It looks almost unnaturally calm from back here," he called out.

Just like the field of flowers did.

Alice knelt to lean over the water's edge just as he had in pursuit of the water bug beside his own pond before coming to Sian.

"How clear my reflection is!" she cried. "It's better than a looking glass!" She dipped her hand into the water. "Oh!" She yanked at her arm awkwardly. "Vincent!"

He finally caught up to her at the shore. "What is it?"

"Something's got me! I can't pull my arm back! I don't believe this is water at all! It's sort of webby, and…." She screamed and lurched forward. Her arm continued to sink jerkily further and further into the pool, just like something on the other side was dragging her in.

"Alice!" He rushed forward and grabbed her free arm, nearly putting his own foot on the glassy surface.

"Vincent!" she screamed. Her face fell beneath the surface.

Vincent still held one hand, but a moment later, the unseen force yanked that from him as well. Duke had hopped down to the shore and stood behind squealing hysterically, and Cyrus still sat on Vincent's shoulder, yelling instructions.

"Alice! Alice!" Vincent realized he'd been screaming right along with the others.

CHAPTER TWENTY-FOUR

Whosoever loves much performs much, and can accomplish much, and what is done in love is done well.

—Vincent van Gogh

Alice stood, pounding on the underside of the surface as if trapped beneath a window. Her mouth moved, but no sound reached Vincent's ears.

Vincent leaned over the pool but dared not touch it. The odd barrier distorted her image, making her appear warped and misshapen. He put a trembling hand to his head.

"Not water at all," he muttered to himself.

"Astute observation, but a little too late, I warrant," the caterpillar said.

"I can do without your remarks!" Vincent's hands balled into tight fists of anxiety, his nails digging grooves in his palms.

Duke bounced back and forth on the shore in a flurry of jittery motion. "Oh, sir! The miss! We've got to do something!"

"I know! I'm thinking!" He grabbed a nearby stick.

Cyrus snorted. "I hardly think that will do any good given the means…"

"Probably not, but I don't hear you coming up with any ideas!" Vincent yelled.

He thrust it through in hopes she could grab it, but as soon as its tip touched the surface, an invisible hand dragged this from him, too.

Like a great pool of quicksand!

The stick fell beside Alice's feet.

"I did think that would happen," the caterpillar said.

"Of course, you did, you insufferable know-it-all. I'm sure you're very good at predicting things that have already happened!"

"But what are we going to do, sir?" Duke wailed.

Vincent exhaled. "I don't know! Either of you have an idea?"

Duke wagged his head mournfully.

"Haven't the foggiest," the caterpillar said. "If your sight was working…." He let the sentence trail off with its implication.

Vincent resisted a very strong urge to throw him into the pond as well. He paced back and forth beside it instead.

Suddenly, a loud squawk just behind his head startled him so badly he nearly fell headlong into the treacherous pool himself. He managed to catch his balance, however, and turned around as quickly as he could.

A huge bird, just taller than Vincent himself, stood behind him. It gave the impression of an uncommonly shabby stork mixed with a flamingo—the latter because it was mostly pink. Gray feathers stuck out all around its head as if it wore a very ratty mop for a hat.

"Lots go in; none come out. Try to warn 'em, but I can't stand here all day, can I? *Rrwawwk!*"

Vincent cringed at the loud screech.

"None come out? Are you sure about that?"

"Quite sure. *Rrwaawk!*"

Vincent shrugged at Alice to indicate he had no idea what to do.

The bird walked up beside him and peered over his shoulder, craning its long neck out over the reflective surface.

"What are you looking at? *Raaawrk!*"

"My friend, of course," Vincent snapped at the bird.

Its eyes widened, and its long neck crooked back in an exaggerated expression of surprise that would've been comical if Vincent had been in the mood for laughing. "You can see her? *Rrwawwk!*"

"Yes! She's right there!" Vincent pointed in frustration.

"I don't see anything except my own reflection. *Rrwawwk!*"

"Must you make that racket after every sentence?" Vincent nearly yelled. It wasn't quite cordial, but his nerves stood on edge already, and that shriek was enough to push anyone over.

"What racket? *Rrwawwk!*" The bird seemed oblivious to Vincent's rudeness.

"Wait a minute." Vincent eyed the bird. "You say you don't see anything?"

"Never do. *Rrwaaak!*"

"You, Duke?" Vincent asked the tove.

"Only my reflection like the bird says! Can you?"

He ignored the question and asked the same of the caterpillar.

"No, I'd no idea you could see any more than we could!" Cyrus answered.

OK, so my regular sight is altered enough for this at least.

He turned back to Alice.

Maybe if she tried finding a way out.

He held out his arms to her and mimed putting on gloves, then pointed to her. She already wore her gloves; he just wanted to remind her of them.

Her eyes got big and she nodded with a grin. Clearly, she hadn't thought of that either.

We're both half in shock.

He watched expectantly as she pressed her hands above her head, apparently touching the barrier, and closed her eyes. But when she opened them a moment later, Vincent read defeat in her face. She shrugged.

"I'm coming in after you," he mouthed, pointing first to himself and then to Alice.

Her eyes grew wide, and she shook her head vigorously.

She demonstrated hitting the surface from underneath as she'd done when she first fell through.

"What else am I going to do?" he yelled, throwing his hands up in frustration but knowing she couldn't hear him. Movement caught his eye, and he saw other creatures approaching Alice beneath the surface.

That can't be good.

But Alice noticed them just as he did and smiled exuberantly as a little crowd of all types of animals drew near.

He shook his head at her undying optimism.

Only her.

She knelt down as if to greet them all one by one.

But then he saw it. A smooth crimson tentacle snaked along the ground, rolling and curling like a tongue, blindly feeling its way nearer the little gathering around Alice.

He gestured wildly, attempting to get her attention, and she finally looked up at him, smiling brightly. He pointed frantically at the horror.

She jumped back when she saw it, ushering all the little animals behind her and standing in front of them.

You stupid, brave girl. My turn, then....

He rammed a resolute hand into his pocket, pulling out the blindfold.

Don't think about it; just do it.

He tied it around his head and stood totally still, feeling very stupid and very hopeless.

Oh please, oh please. Let me see anything at all that would help!

But only blackness greeted him.

Ah, I'm more useless than ever!

He ripped it off.

What am I going to do?

The tentacle crept nearer and nearer the little crowd. It moved like molasses, but the group of animals huddled closer and closer together. Soon, they'd be cornered with nowhere else to go.

And Alice in the front....

CHAPTER TWENTY-FIVE

Success is sometimes the outcome of a whole string of failures.

—Vincent van Gogh

And then he thought of it. Vincent reached above his head and drew the sword from its back sling.

Will it work?

If not, they'd lose the sword as well.

And then what would we do?

They couldn't kill the Jabberwock without it.

I don't care. I can't even find the Jabberwock without Alice. And surely a sword infused with light can handle a strange…well, whatever this is. And maybe she can use it against that thing if it falls through anyway.

He slashed at the smooth surface nearest the shore. The sword came away freely and left a long gash in the murky covering. As soon as the sword broke the seal, a grand cacophony coming from beneath reached his ears.

"Alice!" he yelled.

The expression on her face changed from worry to eagerness.

He hacked again, and another slice opened up in the webbing.

*I'm sure that's what it is now—some kind of web just like she said—*for it came away in little puffs that trailed behind like wisps of smoke.

He slashed again and cut off the top portion of his little fold to cut out a sort of door.

"Come on, come on!" he yelled.

Alice and her little group made a mad dash for the opening. She put herself in the back now, helping all the smaller creatures up to the shore. She finally scrambled up the slope, and Vincent caught her hand and pulled just as the wriggling tentacle snatched like a whip. She screamed as it lashed the back of her leg.

She and Vincent fell into a heap on the shore, but he shot back to his feet. He picked up the sword where it had fallen by his side, ready to do the beast more harm than stealing its prey. But the slithering arm had already retreated far back into its lair.

Birds and beasts alike let out raucous caws and coos and whistles in celebration, and Alice's 'hooray' rang out amidst the rest.

The shabby bird behind him even let out a long, solitary '*Rrwaawwk!*' in apparent celebration. Several small birds flew past Vincent's head, and a number of unidentifiable animals rushed past on the ground.

"I knew you could do it, Vincent!" She hugged him tightly. "And look at all the other animals we saved!" Duke bounded around her feet excitedly. She picked him up and squeezed.

He let out excited little chirrups, though in a moment, he also said, "Not so tight, miss! I'm very happy you're all right, though!"

She put Duke down and looked around the clearing. "And there's one you should meet, Vincent."

"Found a talking one in there, did you?" He smiled at her, elated she was safe.

"Oh, Bill!" she called.

"Right here, ma'am." A lizard-like creature standing up just like a man stepped out from behind a tree. He nodded at Vincent shyly.

"Hello, Bill," Vincent said.

"I named him," Alice whispered.

"I never would've guessed," Vincent whispered back, grinning. "I'm glad you're out of there."

Alice shuddered. "Not as glad as I am."

"So, Bill," Vincent said, "do we know for certain what kind of creature this is?"

Bill wrung his hands and flashed nervous glances between Vincent and Alice.

Alice answered for the little lizard. "He says that arm stretched out every day or so, then grabbed one of the creatures…"—she demonstrated this dramatically—"…and pulled it into a little hole on the side of the pit. I've named it the Bandersnatch, because, you know, it's a sort of band that snatches."

Vincent nodded. "I've an idea it's some kind of worm."

"A worm?" Alice screwed up her face in obvious disgust. "Do you mean that long thing was the whole creature?"

"Maybe," Vincent said. "Who knows? Given the size of this pit, I wouldn't be surprised if that were a tongue or some strange appendage."

Alice grimaced. "So, you think the surface is some sort of silk web like worms make."

"Yes, we know the caterpillar makes it, so...."

"Excuse me!" Cyrus said from Vincent's shoulder. "I'll thank you not to refer to me in the same sentence as that vile beast!"

"Yes, yes." Vincent dismissed it. "I have to say, though, from the sheen on that pit, it must be finer than the grandest silk we can imagine!"

"It'd be worth a fortune if that's true!" Alice said. "But I don't think I'll ever be able to touch a looking glass again without fear of going through it! It felt just like I was being swallowed by that foul webbing." She shivered. "What are we going to do about it, Vincent? We can't leave these little beasts at its mercy."

He frowned.

"Bill,"—Vincent faced the lizard, then his squawking friend—"and...umm...Bird, any ideas?" They greeted him with blank stares just as if neither of them could talk at all. "OK." Vincent nodded, suddenly realizing he might've been rude not to introduce the bird, though he certainly hadn't named it.

It's a bit too late now, though.

"Well, Bird, you said you warned people about the pond but that you couldn't stay here all day, correct?"

"That's right. *Rrwawwk!* Do what I can, though."

He leaned over and whispered to Alice, "Don't talk directly to that bird if you can help it; he can't say anything without adding that awful screech."

Alice grinned.

Vincent looked down at the caterpillar who still sat solemnly on his shoulder, somehow emanating an air of disapproval without saying a word. "Cyrus, you said there is a sort of warning network about the field of flowers, right?"

"To be sure." He nodded.

"Aye!" Bill rocked back and forth on his heels. "We know about that. And everyone already knows to hide from the Jabberwock." His eyes darted every which way as if it may be right beside him. "If they know it's about, anyway."

Vincent spoke to Bill and the bird now, not minding his own advice.

"Could you two send this out the network, too? A warning about drinking from unnaturally still ponds? And until it's well-established, maybe organize a crew to take turns warning others off?"

Bill's countenance brightened at this. "I think we could do, eh, Bird?"

"Could do. *Rrwawwk!*"

Vincent nodded. "That's the best we can do then."

The bird added another shriek for good measure.

Vincent flinched at the noise then smiled at Alice, but her troubled expression remained. "What is it?" he asked.

"Won't the Bandersnatch starve to death if it can't catch its dinner?"

"Oh, Alice!" Vincent said. "Next you'll want to save the Jabberwock! You can't have it both ways."

I'm also fairly certain it will change its hunting tactics and be just fine, but I'll leave that part out.

"I suppose you're right." She sighed. "I don't want any of the other creatures to be eaten, either."

"Exactly. Now, shall we continue on our way?"

"Yes," she said slowly, "but first,"—she looked at Bill—"can you please tell us where we might get a drink and something to eat?"

He led them to a small watering hole nearby. Muddy water rippled in little whorls about its surface.

"It's not as pretty as our last pond, but I daresay this one won't try to eat us," Alice said.

Vincent sighed. "Yes, I suppose we ought not complain."

Bill and the bird scampered away to forage some grub and returned with actual grubs.

Vincent got a good laugh watching Alice attempt polite refusal again, though grubs topped his limits as well.

"Maybe some fruit or nuts...or even seeds?" he said. "If you can find them, of course."

"Oh, we can find 'em," Bill said. He seemed to have shaken off his shyness a little. "But don't you want something with a bit more flavor? No? As you please, then."

"Off we go!" The bird said. "*Rawwwrk!*"

This time, they brought something everyone except Cyrus agreed upon.

"I can find my own dinner, thank you," he said, promptly climbing a nearby bush.

Vincent finally relaxed. He could hardly believe things had come out all right. Still, guilt gnawed at his belly.

I should've known there was something wrong with that pool. I'm sure I would've seen it right off if my sight was working.

"We should be getting on." Alice stood and brushed off her tawny dress, now covered with many smudges of dirt and green patches from sliding down countless mossy embankments.

Vincent's own clothing hadn't fared any better. His dressy white shirt was now a light brown from accumulated grime. He stood with her.

"Yes, I'm as ready as ever." He strode to the bush where the caterpillar rested and made to reach for it.

"I shan't be going," Cyrus said in as patronizing a tone as ever.

Vincent's hand froze in mid-air.

"This quest is doomed," the caterpillar said.

CHAPTER TWENTY-SIX

I often think that the night is more alive and more richly colored than the day.

—Vincent van Gogh

"Doomed?" Alice exclaimed. "Cyrus! You can't mean that!"

"I'm afraid I do." He peered at Vincent scornfully. "I signed up for killing the monster, not walking up on it unawares. If everyone can't be counted on...well...the reward must outweigh the risk to justify endangering my person. I'm a first, as you may know. And it grieves me to say, the current circumstances seem very unfavorable and your chances quite bleak. Take my advice, young lady, and abandon this fool's errand. I heard you say yourself someone told you that you need to practice your gifts to defeat the Jabberwock. Seems if you haven't got one of these gifts at all, you may not fare so well, and neither will anyone near you."

Alice never wavered. "That's your decision, Cyrus, but I'll be going on. Vincent's going to get his sight back, and we're going to kill that Jabberwock."

"Hmph," it said, immediately resuming its leafy meal.

The caterpillar's speech echoed Vincent's own thoughts so closely, he didn't even attempt a rebuttal.

He swallowed a lump rising in his throat. "I understand." He didn't even like the caterpillar, but somehow losing someone in their company made him feel he might as well give up.

Alice said nothing, only took his hand and found their path, Duke scurrying along beside.

Vincent kept very silent for a long time, Alice chattering all the while. The reassuring pressure of her hand in his and her cheerful prattling calmed him even though he only half-listened. He vaguely registered numerous stories about her cat and more about her strange dreams.

He finally spoke, interrupting her mid-sentence. "I'm sorry, Alice."

"For what, Vincent?"

"For what? I've ruined everything. I don't have the sight; the caterpillar left because he can see I'm a failure. The Jabberwock could float up behind us and transform this instant, and I'd never know it was coming!"

"As far as I can tell," Alice said matter-of-factly, "you haven't ruined anything. I'm still here; you're still here; Duke's still here. And Cyrus left! He's not dead. That was his choice, and a cowardly one, too! And we do keep finding it; it's only a matter of time until we kill it!"

Or it kills us.

Vincent kept that thought to himself.

"How can you be so optimistic?"

Her amber eyes crinkled at the edges as she smiled. "What's the use in being otherwise? Will being doubtful help anything? It seems to me that would only make it worse!" She took his arm in hers. "Are you trying to use your vision?"

"I…I am now. I wasn't before."

"Then that's all you can do." She smiled at him. "I believe in you, Vincent. I'm not saying it's going to be easy. In fact, it may be very hard when it comes to the point, but I know you have it in you, whatever it takes."

He couldn't help but smile back despite his fears. "I think you're an angel in disguise, Alice."

She laughed. "Not me. I'm not nearly good enough to be an angel."

The night began to show its colors, and they walked through an open field, sunset blazing through the evening clouds. They both stopped to watch as if under a spell.

A new splash of color streaked across the horizon each minute, reds and yellows converging with clouds reflecting first purple then orange and the blue of the sky.

"It's a magnificent sunset, isn't it, Vincent?"

"Yes, I don't think I've ever seen a better."

"What do you say we stop here for the night?"

Vincent could only nod.

Wonder what that sunset would look like with my other sight.

It struck him this was the first time he'd thought of the sight in a good way since the oyster.

Maybe there's hope for me yet!

As dark slowly overtook the sky, Vincent lay back on the ground, head resting on his hands.

Duke went off to find them something to eat.

Stars peeked through the dwindling dusk one by one, and then, to Vincent's delight, the faint outline of an enormous, red moon glowed above the furthest hill.

"Look, Alice!" He pointed. "It's the first time I've seen a moon here!"

"Beautiful!" she said "Do you think it's always red or just sometimes, like when our harvest moon is low?"

"I guess we'll find out if we lie here long enough."

A peaceful silence fell over them until Alice pointed out a second moon—this one pale orange—dangling over the opposite side of the horizon. "Two moons! Can you imagine?" Her voice was full of delight. "Of course, our wonderland would have two moons! It's perfect."

He laughed, and they fell silent again, the air taking on a magical quality, clouds teasing them with glimpses of the moons as they floated across the sky.

"Are you glad you came here, Alice?" he asked.

"Yes! I would do it again a hundred times over," she said with no hesitation at all. "No matter what happens from here."

"Me, too," he said. And it was true, though his heart trembled at what might yet come. "You know, Alice, this darkness—the sky—is beautiful. It's not empty or lonely or wicked like the Jabberwock. I don't know how to explain it, but compared to that sort of dark, this one is alive, especially with my other sight—the way I described it to you before…like the night itself has a soul."

"Do you think so?" A smile radiated in her voice though the dark hid it from his eyes.

"I do."

"Don't you want to see it again, Vincent? It seems like…like without it, you're missing a piece of yourself."

"Maybe I am. It just seems like too much. When I wore the blindfold or you touched my hand, I couldn't turn it off. Closing my eyes did nothing to tame it. Imagine standing in a room with someone shouting all the time and no way to stop hearing it. It's like that. And what if it got so strong it was like that all the time? If I could snuff it out like a candle, then light it up again when I needed, I don't think I'd mind it."

"I'm not sure gifts work like that, Vincent. How would you know if you needed it? What if you turned it off just before it showed you something magnificent? Or something awful you needed to be ready for? What if I got tired of mine just before we found the Jabberwock? We just have to take things as they come—the good and the bad."

"Yes, I suppose." He sighed.

"You know what I think, Vincent?"

"What?"

"I think you already see everything your gift shows you—just somehow inside your head, like a feeling. And that's why you like to spend hours on your moor or just on your own."

"I never thought of that."

"I'm sure that's it," Alice continued. "And if it is, how would your life really be any different? Except that now you'd know it's real…and wouldn't that be a relief? You'd know why you wanted to get away instead of feeling there must be something wrong with you." Her voice sped up as she got excited. "And you could see horrible people coming and avoid them!" She frowned. "Or could you? Do you think it would work like that?"

He laughed. "I don't know. You're the only person I've seen. But what if you couldn't avoid them? I know good and well you can't just live in a room by yourself all the time, as much as I'd like to."

"Yes, I suppose that's true, but again, you'd feel just the same as you already do…only you'd have your sight to back it up and reassure you that you weren't making it all up in your head!"

"I guess you're right, but it's still hard to imagine."

"Just think about it, Vincent. I think you'll find it's very sensible."

The ground rustled as Duke approached.

"Now," Alice continued, "it's time we moved back to practical matters. What did you bring us for dinner, Duke?"

CHAPTER TWENTY-SEVEN

Great things are done by a series of small things coming together.

—Vincent van Gogh

They woke the next morning with the dawn—the sunrise in wonderland as lovely as its evening counterpart.

Vincent strolled the area, scanning the open field as far as his natural eyes allowed. He even put on the blindfold, but it still revealed nothing. He stuffed it back in his pocket.

The Jabberwock could be anywhere.

A shout from Alice drew him back to the camp.

"Vincent!" she cried as he came over the hill.

He relaxed when he saw only excitement on her face.

"Our Duke is a Duchess! Though I'm not sure I could ever manage to call her anything but 'Duke.'" She waved him over. "Come see! Oh, but they're darling! I've just got to hold one when they wake up."

He leaned over to peer into the little hollow Duke had burrowed the night before. Four tiny, slithery toves nestled next to their "Duke."

He grinned. "A duchess indeed!"

Alice crouched beside Duke and her little family. "Why didn't you tell us you were a duchess instead of a duke?"

The tove looked at her with weary eyes. "I don't know what a duchess is, miss, nor a duke neither!"

Alice laughed. "All right then. Tell us if you need anything."

Duke nodded.

"Let's eat breakfast, shall we?" Vincent said.

"Oh, yes." Alice stood from her stoop. "I am starving."

"You're always starving."

Alice joined him as he pulled out their remaining stores—a few small pieces of fruit and several mushrooms.

"Not a feast, I'm afraid," Vincent said.

"No," Alice sighed. "Adventures don't make for very good eating. That much I've learned."

"That all depends on what you like to eat," a voice said from behind them.

"Oh!" Alice jumped.

The Cheshire cat approached on the side near Duke's little den.

"I do wish you had those bells. If you were Dinah, I would scold you!" Alice said.

Vincent frowned.

Unpleasant little beast. At least I'm my right size this time.

"Just dropping in to be disagreeable again?" he asked.

It flicked its fluffy tail at him, turning its head non-chalantly. "I've only ever been honest, after all!" It strode a few steps nearer Duke and her babies. "It isn't my fault if you didn't take my advice." Its eyes fell on Duke's little hollow. "Well, what have we here?"

Vincent turned back to the food, but something dark and spectral caught his eye. Little tendrils of black seeped from the cat's eyes, curling around its head in obsidian coils.

What....

Alice moved closer to it, and he grabbed her arm.

"Alice, it's...."

And when he touched her, the sight came back full force. The inky horror before him was not a cat. It writhed like a living horde of shadows.

"What is it?" Alice asked.

His grip on her arm tightened, and his breath came in ragged gasps. He only managed a whisper. "That's it...."

"So, you can see me now," the cat said slyly. "I suppose the game is up then."

CHAPTER TWENTY-EIGHT

Only when I fall, do I get up again.

—Vincent van Gogh

It morphed before Vincent's eyes, shooting up and up till it towered over them, three times a man's height. Alice screamed and started toward Duke's nest, but Vincent held her back.

The Jabberwock's terrible eyes glowed with angry fire. "I do like the young ones." It roared, and burbling noises rose from deep within its belly. "And I am hungry."

Vincent reached for the sword, pulling it from the sheath even as the dreadful claws stretched out—each one as long as the sword blade itself.

Duke crouched low over her young, baring her teeth and shrieking with all the fury her little body could hold.

No amount of her will is going to save them.

Vincent made to charge just as Alice pulled free of his grip and dove ahead of him.

"No!" she screamed.

She landed face down, body covering Duke's hollow, shoving Duke out of the way with one hand, and instead of grabbing the toves, the Jabberwock's claws fell on her.

Vincent rushed it, watching in horror as the talons wrapped around Alice's neck. It could have closed its fist about her twice around.

She screamed again, her ragged yell ripping into Vincent's heart. Sword raised, the blood rushing in his ears, he slashed. His blade drew blood from the creature's belly.

It roared, Alice now hanging dreadfully limp in its grasp. It snatched at Vincent with its free hand. He jumped back and raised the sword again, but the monster caught him in a backswing. It flung him across the clearing. He slammed into a tree and slid to the ground, the rough bark tearing gashes in his back. He kept his grip on the sword.

The rabbit's words replayed in his mind: *"If it's got you in its grasp, it's too late."*

But it's Alice! I have to try!

He pushed himself up, ignoring the hot pain searing his back.

I need to be bigger!

He rammed a fist into his pocket and gulped as much cake as his mouth would hold and charged again, still swallowing—choking it down as he ran. He grew larger with each step, nearly as big as the monster by the time he came close enough. He leapt, grasping the sword hilt in both hands to plunge it into the beast, using the momentum of his fall to give it more weight.

I've got it!

The flaming eyes flashed at him, and Vincent smiled in dreadful glee.

I've got you.

He drove the sword down—drove it down into nothing. He landed with a grunt, the sword tumbling uselessly to the ground by his side.

No!

He stood and rounded, expecting the Jabberwock's hot breath on his back, but there was nothing.

"No!" He gasped breaths of dismay, but it was gone.

His giant form towered over the lifeless body that lay on the ground beneath him—Alice's body, old and shriveled as if she'd lived and died a hundred years ago. "Alice!" Tears streamed from his eyes unbidden and unchecked.

He fell to his knees and laid a massive hand on her shrunken cheek. His sight awakened. Even death had not lessened Alice's ability to strengthen his vision. Sooty eddies cloaked her body in darkness, and he wanted to curse himself for his stubbornness.

"No, no. We can fix it. We have to fix it!" He moved to take her hand, now black with age.

I should've seen it; I should have known!

Duke approached from Alice's other side, her face wet with tears. "She saved us. My little babies. Saved us all." The tove wrung her tiny hands together and let out a terrible wail.

A voice boomed from above them, and Vincent jumped.

"There is a way. We can still save her."

As tall as Vincent had grown in his effort to kill the Jabberwock, the old man who stood before him loomed taller. He gazed down at Alice sadly, his white beard floating in the breeze.

Vincent stared, full of grief and shock. Then he exploded. "And who are you? Just watching Alice die from who knows where, waiting to appear when it's convenient for you?" He stood and faced the old man. "Since you act like you know all about it, you could've shown up to help before now. You and the rabbit, too. Where'd he get off to? More important stuff to do than make sure two stupid kids don't die fighting his monster. I...."

The old man reached out and put his hands on Vincent's shoulders. "It is not as simple as you think. It pains me to send one so young, but I cannot go; the Jabberwock would destroy all if he could find me whole. And most cannot see him unless he wishes it. The rabbit has other tasks—"

Vincent started to interrupt, but the old man held a hand up.

"Yes, important ones—tasks that keep the universe on its course. And the battles given to mortals are about more than fighting monsters." He placed a hand on Vincent's chest. "They are battles within, as I think you well know."

This kept Vincent silent. He did know. He had failed his own battle. Alice was dead.

The old gray eyes locked onto Vincent's, and he could not look away. "You were never alone, my boy. Surely you understand that everything cannot be seen—even by you." He drew a pocket watch from his robe and held it in front of Vincent. "Now, we could talk for an age, but Alice needs you before her time runs out."

Vincent took the golden case and noted it was not flat like a pocket watch, but spherical. He opened it.

Not a watch.

An hourglass spun on a gimbal, righting itself within the case no matter how Vincent turned it.

"With your help," the old man continued, "I can save her. I do not do it often, and this time I cannot do it alone, for I no longer hold Alice's time. The creature has stolen it. You must take its head, for her time is stored there, but not for long. It will fade into memory. But with its head, young Vincent, I can restore what has been lost."

"But how will I find the Jabberwock without Alice?"

"Use your gift, child." The old man's voice grew thin. "It is stronger than you know. When the sand runs out, she can no longer be saved. Once you have taken its head, shatter the glass, and I will find you."

"You're Time, then?" Vincent said. "Father Time?" The form wavered, translucent, but he caught a faint nod just before it vanished entirely. He turned back to the object in his hand—the dainty glass curves, gilded and fragile, the sand glinting as it drained, each grain diminishing Alice's chance at life.

Such a beautiful, dreadful object.

Vincent stood over Alice's body.

Use your gift, huh?

He closed the cover on the hourglass and shoved it in his pocket. The velvety blindfold slid across his fingers as if asking him to put it on. He drew it out.

If I ever needed to see, it's now. I don't care what it does to me.

He wrapped it around his head and tied it tight. A pit of emptiness clenched in his stomach. Everything swirled around him as if in a wild whirlwind.

Don't think about it; fix it.

Slate black rivulets rose from Alice's body in the wake of her destruction—the mark of death the Jabberwock left behind. Duke stood just behind her. He'd forgotten Duke.

"I…I can't go, sir," she whimpered. "I can't leave my kits."

"I know, Duke." It somehow seemed fitting that the last chance should come down to him alone. "It's OK."

Cyrus unwilling; Duke unable; Alice dead. There's only me.

"It's OK." And this time, he said it to himself.

He knelt and placed his hand on Alice's arm.

Where are you, Jabberwock?

Every fiber of his being wanted to find the creature and take its head. He'd never wanted his gift so badly. He didn't let the vision cloud his mind.

Look at it from the outside like Alice said. Focus.

The muddied vortex in his mind cleared, and he found he could see further than his vision had ever allowed before. He stood still, but it felt as if he were speeding through the forest, ethereal trees streaking past him in whirlpools of light. Then came a jolt, like a needle of ice piercing his heart. He gasped. The Jabberwock's jet-black form hovered in a clearing halfway through the forest. It stood out in raw clarity, devilish and cruel. He could see its soul— the antithesis of the rabbit. Atralius had been all light, teeming with vibrant energy; this creature lived on the blackness of death—a terrible empty horror draining the color from everything near it, a vast depth of nothing opening onto this wonderland.

Alice's wonderland.

CHAPTER TWENTY-NINE

I am seeking, I am striving, I am in it with all my heart.

—Vincent van Gogh

Rage coursed through Vincent's veins. He picked up the sword where it had fallen and sheathed it in its scabbard, then he ran. He ran through the forest with more purpose than he'd ever felt in his life. Whatever happened, no matter his fear, he couldn't hesitate. He had to do this, and he had to do it fast. His bloody back shot with pain at every step, but it only drove him on. He found the mad rush of color easier to navigate than he had imagined. Tiny ripples in the air and light told him to dodge, to jump, to duck.

His giant strides gained good ground, his head only just beneath the tallest line of trees. A rainbow of animals drifted below him as he fled—animals normally camouflaged in the leaves swirled with light, as visible to him as fish swimming in a clear pond. He ignored them. He ignored anything that wouldn't help get Alice back.

And then something living flashed directly across his vision. Its form trembled in yellows and greens and he felt it fall on his shoulder.

Cyrus.

"How did you get here?" Vincent panted the words but did not stop his run.

"Came to find you." It spoke as imperiously as ever. "Through the trees. I saw you coming and dropped on your shoulder. My, how large you are." Its words shook with Vincent's footsteps. "I felt ashamed of my cowardice—sending little girls off to fight monsters and forsaking duty in order to save myself. Where is she by the by?"

"Dead," Vincent said. "For now."

He offered no more elaboration, and the caterpillar asked for none.

The running did Vincent good and when he grew near enough to slow, a purposeful calm had taken root, replacing his reckless anger.

"I need to think—" he said to Cyrus, "to make a plan."

"Yes," the caterpillar agreed.

Vincent began pacing and talking to himself more than to the caterpillar. "I can see it, but that's not enough. The rabbit said it must be in its feeding form to be killed. I can't just get there and look at it! What am I going to do?"

"Ahem." Cyrus cleared his throat in his absurd way. "I may be of some assistance. I may have mentioned, I am a *first,* and..."—it paused—"it really can't resist...firsts." Its voice trembled as it spoke this last word. It cleared its throat again, and not with a silly "ahem," to garner attention.

Vincent eyed the caterpillar closely.

Cyrus began again. "I've seen it feed, you know. Goes into a sort of frenzy. I really don't think it would be able to help itself."

Vincent examined the tiny creature on his shoulder, its yellow-green aura shot through with blue.

Is that fear? Courage? Both?

"Are you saying what I think you are?" he asked.

"If what you think is that I will draw it out for you, then...yes." The caterpillar looked away.

He wants to be humble, now that he's finally doing something to be proud of.

"You would do that?" Vincent asked. "Offer yourself as bait?"

"I'll not die a coward hiding in a mushroom, anyway," it said in answer. "You can get the little girl back, then?"

"If I'm quick enough," Vincent said. He pulled the hour glass out of his pocket and pressed the button for the cover. "Before this runs out." He showed the caterpillar.

Over half the sand gone already.

It nodded concisely. "Then we'd best be off. Where is it?"

"Just ahead."

"Right. Then get me as close as you can without it knowing we're there and let me down. I'll approach it and then you kill it when it…umm…and then we'll be rid of it. Jolly good."

Its antennae quivered slightly.

"Thank you," Vincent said.

It nodded curtly.

Vincent pulled out his last vial of tea. "I've got to shrink again, though. I can't sneak up at this size."

He drank about half and waited till he stopped shrinking.

Not quite enough.

He took another gulp and came close to his natural size. He took a deep breath and headed for the clearing, stepping as silently as possible. He approached behind some brush. The dark mass rippling in the center filled him with dread.

"You can't see it, can you?" he whispered to the caterpillar.

"No." Its voice was barely a peep.

"It's there in the middle. I'm right behind you."

He lowered Cyrus to the ground and drew the sword noiselessly from its sheath.

The caterpillar straightened up a little, seeming to draw courage from the sight of it. Vincent understood. It crawled out into the open grass without another word. Vincent crept around the edge of the clearing to approach the Jabberwock from behind.

The undulating shape sharpened in Vincent's mind's eye, then its smoky edges stretched and shifted.

Its blazing eyes showed first, two red blotches in a cavernous void, then its claws sprung forth, attached to nothing, and its wings burst into existence. Death being born.

The Jabberwock roared, and Vincent could see Cyrus trembling, tiny tremors of blue emanating out from him like heat waves.

"Well, well." The gravelly voice of the Jabberwock sounded so different from the smooth wheedling of the Cheshire cat. "I thought I'd gotten all the firsts, but there are always a few stragglers."

Vincent put a hand in his right pocket. His heart clenched. It was empty. The remaining crumbs of cake fell through his fingers as he drew his hand out.

I can't even reach its head from this height!

He squeezed his fist.

It doesn't matter. The size didn't help last time.

The Jabberwock bent, and as it dove for Cyrus, Vincent charged.

He slashed at the back of its knees, and it bellowed, legs buckling. Vincent rolled beneath its immense talons as they severed the very air above his head. The monster rocked unsteadily on its wounded legs.

Please fall.

Then it flapped its terrific wings, and Vincent saw it meant to fly.

No, no, no.

He rushed it, not pausing to think, turning his back on that dreadful head. He targeted a wing.

I won't get another chance. Alice won't get another chance.

A roaring cry thundered above him. The air roiled and writhed around Vincent's head, and he found he could read the Jabberwock's every move in the rushing whorls as clearly as if he observed the battle from above. It had delayed its flight and poised to strike at his back, thinking him easy prey.

It doesn't know I can see it.

It lunged—teeth gleaming, deadly jaws hurtling toward him from behind.

This is it.

He continued headlong towards its wing, pretending to be unaware.

Not yet.

His every step fell with a rasping breath of terror, and sweat dripped down his back, stinging his wounds, but he waited—waited until the dragon's hot wind billowed across his neck.

CHAPTER THIRTY

Love is something eternal; the aspect may change, but not the essence.

—Vincent van Gogh

He feinted, dodged, and swung the sword around with all his might.

A terrible gurgling cry filled the air. Vincent fell to the ground, and a mighty, crushing weight pinned him to the earth. He panicked.

I'm dead. I'm dead. I'm dead.

But as he clawed the dirt to escape its grasp, he saw the Jabberwock's severed head staring at him with empty, dead eyes. Only its lifeless body held him down.

A cry of relief escaped him, and he reached for the hourglass, but the Jabberwock's massive bulk lay across him. Vincent's pocket—and the hourglass within it—were trapped beneath.

His relief turned to anguish, and he groaned.

Even in your death, you will win!

Hot tears of rage and despair coursed down his cheeks. He strained with every muscle in his body, pushing his hand beneath the monster. He dug his nails into the dirt, opening a path, gaining one inch, then another, then another. His fingers touched the tips of his pocket and finally, the cool metal of the hourglass case. He yanked his arm back, the Jabberwock's scales scraping skin from his arm. He popped open the cover of the hourglass—the merest traces of sand still falling.

No time to waste.

He pressed his thumb into the glass, and it cracked, turning the grains red with his blood.

A shadow fell instantly, and Father Time stood above him in white majesty, sending ripples of blazing light in terrific motion around his body.

"You've slain the Jabberwock, my boy!"

He laughed raucously as if all the world were a delight, but Vincent did not join him.

"Alice! We've got to get back to Alice!"

"Yes, but now we've got its head, we need not hurry."

He placed his hand above the Jabberwock's head, and thousands of many-colored ribbons trailed through the air like shooting stars.

"I have her time in my hand, young Vincent, and can preserve it as I like." He smiled. "Now, let's get you free."

The old man rolled the Jabberwock's body away as if it weighed nothing at all, and Vincent groaned in pain and relief.

Father Time bent and hunted around his feet. "There is another I need to find, however."

He reached his gleaming fingers to the ground and parted the grass gently.

"Ahh! Here you are."

A little yellow-green haze lay in the old man's hand. *Cyrus.*

"Is he all right?" Vincent asked.

"Not dead anyway," Time said, "but I think the creature managed to take a little of me from him. How do you feel, my friend?"

The caterpillar rolled his face toward Time. "A bit done up, but, as you said, not dead."

It certainly sounded weary to Vincent's ears.

"Luckily, friend," Father Time said, "your time is as fresh as ever and I hold it here, thanks to young Vincent." He touched his finger to the caterpillar's head and several tiny streaks of light passed between them.

Cyrus took in a deep breath. "Much better." He bowed formally. "Profoundly obliged to you, sir."

Vincent watched this with much impatience but held his tongue. He realized he still wore the blindfold and ripped it off. But removing it changed nothing at all. The world billowed around him in rushing waves, his special sight as strong as it had ever been. He froze, not even breathing, trying to grasp this new reality. He was still in shock when the old man spoke.

"Now, shall we go revive young Alice?"

"Yes!" Vincent sputtered with a raspy exhale. He began walking without a word. His back throbbed, his scraped arm burned, his legs trembled as he walked, and his heart faltered thinking about his transmuted sight, but he would not delay Alice's revival for anything in the world.

When they reached her, he stooped by her side and took her blackened hand in his once more.

Father Time drew near and reached a finger to Alice's forehead, but before he touched her, he looked at Vincent.

"I think, young master, she would do better to forget this."

"You can do that?" Vincent asked.

"Yes, but would you have me?"

"Yes, I don't want her to remember becoming…"—he looked back down at her—"…becoming this."

"But I cannot choose so carefully. If she does not remember this, she will not remember any of it, except as in a dream."

Vincent's heart dropped. "You mean, she won't remember me."

"I'm afraid not."

Hot tears welled. Vincent remembered how Alice's color had dimmed when they got lost. He thought of how the Jabberwock had tainted the oyster and how Alice herself had changed as it yelled in anger. It terrified him to think of her faded and dull, or worse—empty and black. He couldn't risk it. He couldn't bring her back to darkness. He nodded. "It's better."

Father Time placed a hand on his shoulder. "Very good. I will return her to her home." He touched his finger to Alice's forehead. Shots of red and orange and white streamed from his finger.

It flooded Alice's body like lightning, every bit of her majesty returning in a maelstrom of color. Everything churned in a tumult of whirls and garlands of light. And this—watching Alice's life given back to her—was the most sublime vision yet. Shining brightness and energy replaced every spot of black and death seeping from her—restoring her colors in front of him. He wept with joy at the breathtaking beauty of Alice's life returning, but also with sorrow because he would never see her again. The color spread across her body, and he watched as she aged backwards, the old Alice's colors steady and full, stately and peaceful, middle-aged Alice, light and energetic, happy and rested, and back to his young Alice, full of fire. Then she faded from his sight forever.

Duke approached with all four of her blind little kits clasping tightly to her back the same way Alice and Vincent had done down the stream.

"Hello, Duke," Vincent smiled. "So, riding us down the river was good practice, I suppose."

"Yes, sir." Duke nodded and looked at the empty place where Alice had been moments before. "The miss... she was a lady, wasn't she, sir?"

Vincent stooped. "She was the very best lady."

Duke reached out and put a paw on his hand. "I just wanted to say I'm glad it all came out right. I knew you and the miss would protect us."

"I'm glad it all came out right, too," Vincent said.

Father Time smiled and turned to Cyrus, who he'd placed on Alice's other side. "And we are not done with you, Sir Caterpillar. I've a message for you from on high. Your sacrifice will never be forgotten. For your service today, you and all your descendants will be blessed with a beauty more delicate and elaborate than any other creature in Sian. You will always begin as a caterpillar because that is where you found your honor, but you shall grow into something magnificent and trade your crawling feet for glorious wings."

"Thank you, sir." Cyrus bowed, and Vincent noted that the caterpillar did not seem the slightest bit pompous now.

"Vincent," Father Time said, "you also have done a great service, not only to this world and to Alice, but to me." He bowed a deep bow. "I thank you, young sir. Now, to return you home as well…."

The blurry outlines of Vincent's feet were insubstantial, the navy of his shoes bleeding into the brown of the dirt around them.

He gathered his courage, though a bit daunted by the imposing figure of Father Time. "Could I make a request? I know it's bold of me to ask, but I only…since the caterpillar got a reward…."

"Yes, Vincent. Do not be afraid."

"Will my sight go back to normal in my world? Or can you make it do so?"

A twinge of dark blue flowed through the old man's light.

Sadness.

"Your vision is your reward, young Vincent. Your world will subdue it a little, but it is your gift. Do you see it as a burden?"

"I just...I don't know how I'll stand it. The things I'll see...." He remembered the horrible darkness of the Jabberwock. "I'm afraid of the darkness in people... and the emptiness. I'm already not like anyone else, and this...I don't think I'd ever be able to pretend."

"Gifts are given not only for the good of the bearer, child," Father Time said. "I do not say that all gifts are easy, but they all exist for a good bigger and greater than you can know. Would you deny the world something only you can give and deny yourself the chance to give it?"

"I don't know, sir." Vincent shuffled his feet in the dirt. "Will it be worth it?"

"It is always worth it, though you may never know it in your lifetime, for ripples go out and out forever from every bit of love given and every hardship endured for the good of others. I have seen from the dawn of all worlds as each gift embraced rides on and on into the future like a wave." Father Time stared into Vincent's eyes. "I can take the gift from you if that is what you choose—if your heart's desire is to fade, unnoticed, into your own world and live in ease. But is that truly what you wish?"

Vincent thought about this, imagining the gifts flowing out like waves, like the ripples each tiny beetle caused on the pond at home—a pond that seemed still and untouched unless you watched it carefully. Alice had said he would lose his own color by trying to hold back his sight.

And she was right. I knew it all along.

"No," he sighed. "I suppose I don't really wish to give it up. So many people seem to fade, so as not to see the world or other people or even themselves. They live afraid and trying to do what everyone else expects, and they end up not living at all. They lose…the bigness…all the things that really matter."

Time's color ran with strands of pink now, and Vincent knew he was smiling.

His hand touched Vincent's shoulder yet again. "Then show them the 'bigness,' young Vincent. There are few who can."

Vincent nodded.

"Now, let's get you home, boy," Time said, putting his finger to Vincent's forehead.

Vincent had no memory of returning to the barrow mound on the moor, nor of getting back into his own clothes, nor of his wounds healing, but everything else remained as clear as any memory from his own world. And if he doubted, stepping back through the brush onto the moor put those doubts to rest. Its beauty struck him as never before. The colors seemed alive, running from one place to another and back again, traipsing their light into shadows and drawing little swirls in their dance. At each step he took, the very ground rippled beneath him. He walked all the way home entranced with this new magic.

He reached the back stoop of his house before he recalled any troubles.

I've lost my jar.

And then he smiled.

Guess that means I'll have to go out looking for it tomorrow.

EPILOGUE

It is precisely in learning to suffer without complaining, learning to consider pain without repugnance, that one risks vertigo a little; and yet it might be possible, yet one glimpses even a vague probability that on the other side of life we'll glimpse justifications for pain.

—Vincent van Gogh

London, England – 1873

"London does not suit," Vincent muttered to himself as he made his way into work. "Too close; too dim."

He rented a room in a cottage as far from town as he could find, though this meant a steam-boat journey and a long walk in to work every morning.

"I need the space," he told his family. They complained it would keep him away from society and was far too inconvenient. "I need the trees and the fields. London is shrouded in an incessant cloud."

He'd been reassigned from his place in The Hague.

Can't manage the patrons, they say. That's because the patrons have no taste!

He strode into work, the gray oppression of the town already weighing on him. The crowds overwhelmed him, their fear and anger and passion clearly visible in the colors that trailed around their bodies. He just needed to get away from it sometimes. Thus, the cottage.

He normally worked in the back room of his uncle's art shop, cataloguing and organizing, but an onslaught of customers occasionally brought him to the front. Such was the case today.

The sour-faced, aristocratic woman led him to the piece that drew her interest. He could tell by looking at her they weren't going to get on. He never mixed well with gray people, and she was swathed in it, a sooty fog trailing behind her every step. He'd discovered that gray people seemed to have dulled themselves intentionally, as if it were somehow indecent to stand out.

"I'd like something sylvan that gives an idea of space, you know," she said. "What is the price on this one?"

Wouldn't know sylvan if it hit her on the head. That one's got all the beauty of a butter knife.

"You'll not want that one, though, surely." Vincent knew she wouldn't take his advice but couldn't help giving it. He never could. "The colors are all wrong."

He led her to another section—one he'd arranged with his favorites.

The ones that actually mean something.

"These, madam, are infinitely more pleasing to the senses."

She wrinkled her nose. "Young man, those will never do. So gauche! They assault the senses rather than tickle them."

She took hold of another clerk recently freed from the clutches of his shopper and led him over to the piece she'd initially asked about.

Vincent stood, shoulders stooped, hoping he could return to the warehouse in the back now, when someone touched his arm, and the world lit up in a way it hadn't since....

Alice.

She stood before him, nearly as tall as he was, ribbons of red and orange dancing around her.

"You were quite right, you know." She did not wait for him to speak. "The one she'd chosen is absolutely abysmal—as if someone doused the landscape with ash."

His tongue did not respond to his commands, but Alice seemed not to notice and carried the conversation on her own.

"And that makes me think you're just the person to help me." She faced the pieces he'd recommended. "Show me your absolute favorite."

He led her silently to a small landscape awash with sunlight, beams shooting between trees across the greenest of fields. A man stood on a hill at the edge of the painting, revealing only his back as he surveyed the beauty of the field below.

Alice smiled a little half-smile at him. "That's the one. I knew you were the right person to ask. I've a knack for finding just what I'm looking for, you know…or just the person to help me find it." She released his arm and picked up the small painting. "The man here, standing alone amidst all this wondrous beauty…."

"Do you think it's important that he's alone?" Vincent interrupted, finally finding his voice.

"Oh, it's imperative," Alice said. "This man is still discovering. We don't know what, but that's why it's lovely. He could be dreaming about absolutely anything! But putting someone else in the painting with him would demolish any wistful contemplation. Put a lady by his side and the whole scene becomes a common romance, all the brilliance excused as young love. Everything would be wrapped up in his infatuation, of course, and nothing left to wonder about at all!"

Vincent started to speak, but she continued.

"And if you put a man there, it all becomes dull and business-like. I'm sure this is very unfair to men, but don't they often become like that when they're together—as if it's shameful to be any other way? They're bound to be talking of how to make the best use of the land and what to plant or where to graze or whether to sell and which trees to cut down and ignoring its beauty altogether.

She examined his face. "But I don't think that would be the case if you were one of the men. You can't ignore the beauty if you try, can you?"

His cheeks burned, and she peered at him intently.

"No," she said. "I thought not. You know, I think you are the man in this painting, destined to do something wonderful, only still discovering what that is."

"Do you think so?" he asked. "But, how could you? You don't even know me."

"Ah, but I told you I was good at finding things, and my skill extends just a little further than one may expect." She held her hand out to him. "Give me your hand. It's even stronger when I hold someone's hand." She giggled. "And I suppose I should introduce myself before I go asking for a man's hand. "I'm Alice."

He took her hand. "Vincent," he said.

A brief bewilderment passed across her face like a cloud. "Why, I feel we know each other, Vincent, or like we met in a dream. I have very vivid ones, you know." She shook her head as if to clear it. "But no matter. Back to my finding."

She closed her eyes and scrunched up her face just the way Vincent remembered, then opened them and released his hand. Her smile exploded in to the rays of light, sending swirls of color radiating in every direction.

"Yes, Vincent," she said. "You're quite extraordinary, and don't let anyone tell you otherwise."

"But what am I to do?" he asked.

"I'm afraid it's not that specific, Vincent." She shook her head. "But don't you give up. No matter what."

Footsteps resounded behind her and Vincent looked up into the face of a man nearly his own age but several inches taller.

"Hello! I think Alice is teasing you with her fancies." He put a possessive hand on her shoulder. "People have other things to do, my dear, and you're keeping this gentleman from his work." The young man held his hand out, smiling broadly. "Thank you for your assistance."

Vincent searched the man's expression and found no ill-will. He took the offered hand. He examined all the swirls and eddies for any reason to doubt the man's honor but couldn't find one. Steady blue lines fell around him like a uniform.

He smiled at the man with some difficulty. "It's not a problem, I assure you. I was just helping the young lady find a painting that suited her."

Alice held it up proudly. "Isn't it lovely?"

"Very nice, yes. Now, we must be off. Thank you for your help, sir."

He nodded at Vincent and ushered Alice away.

Vincent stood watching for many minutes—well after they'd paid and their silhouettes blended in with the throng of people in the street. A sharp tap on the shoulder finally broke the spell.

"Vincent!" His manager stood behind him. "What are you doing? The shop's cleared out, and you can go back to your regular duties."

Vincent nodded and walked away in a sort of trance. He remembered Alice calling him extraordinary once before, her young voice echoing in his mind: "To be extraordinary is, by definition, to be something other than ordinary. And if one isn't ordinary, I'm afraid one might very often feel out of place."

And all the myriad of swarming colors blurred into tears he could not hold back as he returned to his desk.

But I haven't given up, Alice.... I haven't.

The End

AUTHOR'S NOTE

It goes without saying that this book would never have been written if it weren't for two of the most beloved creatives of the nineteenth century—Lewis Carroll and Vincent van Gogh. I can only hope I have not done them a disservice with my tribute.

Oddly enough, I did not begin this book intending to do a retelling. In my first book, *The Worlds Next Door*, which takes place far into the future of Sian (Wonderland), the main character realizes that Vincent van Gogh had experienced what she was experiencing. When I wrote that sentence, I did not intend for it to be anything but a passing thought. The idea that I could actually bring Vincent's story into the world grew later, and when I say grew, I mean it grew like a weed. I was a fair bit into the sequel for *The Worlds Next Door*, but I just wasn't feeling it.

Then one night I had one of those creative insomnia fits where the ideas roll in and keep you up all night (or at least until 4:00 AM), and I couldn't stop thinking about what might've happened if Vincent entered Sian. I still had no inkling of including Wonderland. But in the few hours of sleep I did get that night, I dreamed I had a talking rabbit with one ear. It didn't strike me that this was related to Vincent until later, and even when it did, I thought, "Well, a rabbit could greet him in Sian. It would be a nice nod to *Alice* in the same way *The Worlds Next Door* had a few subtle nods to *Peter Pan.*"

That's as far as I took the Wonderland connection until I actually started writing. Alice wouldn't stop popping into my head. I kept imagining what she might say here or how she and Vincent would get along or what may happen if I really did intend to set the story in Wonderland. And when I looked up "Alice Liddell" (Lewis Carroll's real-life inspiration for *Alice's Adventures in Wonderland)* and found she was born just one year earlier than Vincent, there was no turning back. Sian was Wonderland and that was that.

I hope the story was as fun for you to read as it was for me to write. I know I've had a few readers note the conspicuous absence of the Mad Hatter, the Red Queen, and the March Hare. The first two were left out partially because the intelligent species had not yet been created in Sian. Mostly, they were all left out because they didn't seem to fit in Vincent's story, which was my focus. If I'd been writing Alice's, I'm sure they would have appeared. I did have one reader who suggested that Vincent *is* the Mad Hatter in my story. This idea delighted me, but alas, it was not mine. Perhaps we can infer that in Alice's telling of the story when she returns to the real world, Vincent becomes the Mad Hatter in her dream-memory of events.

Thank you for reading, and if you are so inclined, please leave a review of *Vincent in Wonderland* on Amazon, Goodreads, or your preferred platform. Reviews are the lifeblood of independent authors, and I will take your honest, kindly stated opinion to heart even if it is negative.

Be extraordinary, fellow wayfarers, and never give up.

You can find more adventures in C.E. White's first book, *The Worlds Next Door,* which is available on Amazon.com.

Go to the author's website to sign up for her newsletter and keep up with future works:
www.cewhitebooks.com

You can also follow C.E. White on social media at the following links:
www.instagram.com/cewhitebooks
www.facebook.com/cewhitebooks
www.twitter.com/cewhitebooks

If you've enjoyed *Vincent in Wonderland,* please share with your friends, and take a moment leave a review on Amazon, Goodreads, or your preferred platform. It doesn't have to be long. Even just your star rating with a one-word entry is helpful!

Reviews have an incalculable impact on future readers, especially for independent authors.